I0662240

The Bond

Michele Majors

Published by Miancy House, 2022.

Copyright

First edition September 2021

Cover Design by James, GoOnWrite.com[1]

ISBN 979-8-98686-640-6 (print)

ISBN 978-0-578-95448-6 (ebook)

michelemajors.com[2]

Table of Contents

With Love:

FOR

Daddy and Momma

FOR

Angie, Michael, and Chauncey

AND FOR

Eric

The Bond

The man I met at the club told me I wanted to die.

I spotted the man on the other side of the club. The flashing red, white, and purple lights shined on his face as he approached me, and the silver and white strobe light created the illusion of slowed motion. He looked like a god posing for the photographers' flashing cameras. I tilted my head to look up at the handsome man with the chiseled face and groomed goatee. He looked like a god the way his black turtleneck hugged his chest and stomach. His black slacks revealed a thin waist over strong legs.

"You called me," he said, revealing straight white teeth against his ebony skin.

"Excuse me?" I said my head bobbing to the music.

"You were waiting for me, and I have searched for you. I saw you watching me," he said taking my hand. "You want to die to all of this," he said and pointed his free hand to the mass of dancing bodies on the dance floor. "You have a death wish. Let me take you there."

"What?" I stared at him, but he refused to repeat himself. I continued bobbing my head to the music and studied his kissable mouth. How would his lips feel on my skin?

Denise.

"They call me Greg. Tell me your name."

None of these people knew me. They were beautiful but flawed and I wanted protection. No one knew me at this nightclub or at least I never told anyone my real name, but I clearly heard my name whispered in a man's voice that sounded like the god-man in front of me. I took a sip from my drink and put it down.

"Denise."

"Denise." He said my name again and seemed to savor the way my name rolled on his tongue.

I glanced around the club, and the patrons stared more closely at this god-man in front of me. The crowd never changed. Men carrying condoms in their wallets hoped tonight they would be lucky enough to meet a woman who had her own place and who had no ex-boyfriend or father of a child hanging around on the side of the street waiting for the mother of his child to bring a man home. And the women hoped even as they dabbed more lipstick on their mouths and dusted their faces with powder again that this night, they might meet a man who stimulated them with his smile, his conversation, his commitment — a relationship and maybe sex.

The crowd never changed except tonight. The god-man standing before me flashed like a red and green and purple neon sign, and his mouth spoke music and a language that rolled from his lips like diamonds. His beauty framed him enveloping him like some men's fragrant cologne that clung to his skin like his color — permanent. Beauty covered him like Texas winter rain painting newly paved roads shiny and wet. I knew he was flawed but felt his presence changed the crowd's dynamic. The hunger in his eyes for me signaled that the crowd at least tonight remained no longer the same.

He took me in his arms, and we danced on a fast-paced song that sounded like a remix of a back-in-the day classic by Jodeci, but he insisted on creating his own lover's dance, and slowed our movements to one of a slower tempo song. The dancers around us appeared as blurred Monet images, and I loved it. Greg gyrated his hips against mine and spun me around. He pressed my body close to him, his scent mingled with my own, and my skin burned at his touch.

"You have a death wish, Denise," he whispered wind on my cheek and again in my ear. "And I can take you to that place."

I ignored his comment and danced with him. I enjoyed the way my body molded to his body; his burning touch weakened and excited me. Perhaps the wine I had consumed earlier in the evening now played tricks with my head and my body. Ending our dance, he took his business card and placed it in my palm. "Call me when you need me," he said and left me standing alone on the dance floor.

The other men in the nightclub who had watched us whispered their promises of forever while I strolled past. Earlier in one man's car, I asked him for forever, and he thought forever meant the short interlude in his red Mitsubishi bucket seats. Wiping my tears and pulling down my skirt, I wanted forever and once again, a man's words fell on the wind. These men only smiled, but Greg, a god, heard my call, my need, and answered me.

I can take you to that place.
I called him the next day.

—————◆—————

OPENING MY EYES TO a dimly lit room, I glanced at the nightstand and saw the clock's red numbers, which read two a.m. I sat up in bed, and my head throbbed. I removed the covers from the bed and saw Greg in bed next to me. I glanced at Greg's back and staggered into the bathroom. The bathroom's vanity had a small handheld bronze mirror covered with traces of white powder. I took a shower.

I left the shower and screamed when I saw the skeleton staring at me from the mirror. Red, white, and purple lights flickered around the skeleton whose sunken cheeks stretched against its skull. Its darkened teeth smiled at me. No lips hid the grimace. Red splotches covered the skeleton's bare head. The skeleton laughed, and I covered my ears backing away from it. I blinked, and the skeleton disappeared.

I ran to the bed and shook Greg. "Greg, I need something. I'm seeing things again." My hands trembled, and my head hurt.

"In a minute, Denise," he said, covering his head with a pillow. "You're having a trip, a release. Flow with it."

"No, now. I need it now." I glanced around the darkened room and switched on the lamp. "I don't like this trip."

Greg removed the pillow from his head, reached under the bed, and retrieved a black toiletry bag. He unzipped the black toiletry bag and removed a wrapped plastic syringe and glass vial filled with liquid. He held the syringe and glass vial in his hands. He sat up in bed.

"How badly do you want it?" he asked, revealing a smile through his goatee.

"Look, just give it to me." I paced back and forth in front of him and rubbed my arms.

"How much this time, Denise?"

"Add it to my bill."

"Do you want me to shoot you up?"

"I'll do it myself." I grabbed the plastic syringe and glass vial of liquid and walked to the bathroom.

I sat on the toilet seat. I wrapped the elastic tubing around my upper arm and tapped the inside of my arm several times until veins appeared. I inserted the needle and closed my eyes when the liquid entered my body. I moaned.

———•———

I LOOK AT GREG AND see the red, white, and purple lights again. Music bounces in my head.

I close my eyes and the purple surrounds me like a lover, and I reach out to that lover, and he takes me never letting me go, and I smile. Greg's so kind. He plays my colors, my song, my music. He loves me like a puppy wanting to be petted, walked, and loved like me.

———•———

GREG OPENED THE BATHROOM door wearing a navy-blue hooded robe. He walked over to me and lifted me from the toilet seat.

"I love you, Greg," I said. I leaned against him, and he marched me from the bathroom to the bed. He removed my robe and revealed my naked body. I sat down. "Do you want me again, Greg?" I stood up, wiggled my hips in a seductive dance, and fell onto the bed.

He stared at me.

"Greg, come to me. I need you," I said. I reached my arms up to him. The white, red, and purple lights that surrounded him flickered to the music beat. I narrowed my eyes to focus on him, but he moved. I giggled.

"Denise."

"Yes," I said. "Greg stop ... moving. You're messing ... with the lights."

Greg fell onto the bed next to me and stroked my stomach with his longer slender hands. I closed my eyes.

"Denise, I'm going home now. You stay here and sleep this off."

"What? I'm not ... high. There's nothing wrong except I'm a little ... horny now." I placed my hands around his neck, but he removed my hands and placed them on my stomach. I giggled again.

Greg disappeared. He returned from his shower dressed in his black slacks and matching black wool turtleneck. Pulling his black leather coat on, Greg walked by the bed and stared at me again.

"Why do you always have to leave? Can't you stay?" I asked.

"You know how to reach me." He placed his card on my stomach and walked away to the door. A hunger lingered in his dark brown eyes, and a burning sensation spread from my stomach throughout my body. I sank into the white sheets that enveloped me like a shroud.

"Aren't you going to kiss me goodbye?"

He stopped at the door a moment. Strolling back to the bed, Greg leaned down and kissed me on the lips. His cologne mingled with my skin. He released me and covered my body with the white sheets and red blanket. The door slammed, and I sniffed the sheets that carried his scent.

———◈———

LATER THAT MORNING, I woke from my slumber. I stepped out of bed and passed two empty wineglasses and an empty wine bottle on the floor. I glanced at the clock's red numbers, which read six-thirty a.m.

I looked into the closet and found a pair of black slacks and a red sweater. I pulled on my boots and my wool coat. I left my house with my purse and briefcase but returned to find my missing car keys. Crawling on the floor, I found the keys wrapped up in a green G-string under the bed. I grabbed the keys and left.

I flew down Interstate 20, the haven of truckers it seemed, in the red BMW that Greg gave me for my thirty-eighth birthday last year. I weaved between cars on the freeway.

Ten minutes later, I exited the freeway and slowed down in the residential neighborhood. Yellow school lights flashed off and on within the school zone, and my car crept along. Finally, I entered the teacher's parking lot, parked my car, and hurried to my freshman homeroom class.

I glanced at my classroom clock, which read seven-thirty in the morning. My students arrived at eight-thirty a.m. I had time to review my lesson plan for Monday. Before reviewing the lesson plan book, I opened my orange lipstick tube and inserted my baby finger in the tube retrieving my coffee — another one of Greg's gifts to me — and sniffed the white powder up my nose.

———◈———

I RAN OUT OF STUFF early Friday morning. I paged and called Greg starting at six a.m. all day Friday, but he never returned my calls. I called his Blackberry at six-thirty a.m. I sent him a text message at seven a.m. I called his Blackberry at seven-thirty a.m. and eight-thirty a.m. When my students took their history test, I texted him again. Damn. Why hadn't he called me yet? He checked that stupid fancy PDA of his religiously for emails, text messages, and voice mails. How many times had we spent time together when he thumbed his fingers across the tiny keyboard like a video game? Too many times.

Later that afternoon I watched the white clock on my classroom wall more closely than my students watched the white clock. The black hands connected to the dots and numbers in slow motion. The red hand circled the clock like a pulse. Beat. Tick. Beat. Tick. Beat. Tick. It matched my heart.

My students chattered among themselves about going to the football game, the movies, and the mall. While they planned their weekend, I left my desk and stood in the hallway against the brown door to my classroom. Other freshman teachers paced the hallway. Some teachers chatted about their weekends, which meant grading papers and helping their children with homework.

They all wanted their weekend, and I wanted my lover.

I began to pace in the hallway too. I stuck my head in the classroom for a moment, and my class lowered their weekend planning voices to hushed whispers.

The clock's hands moved like two dancers in a waltz. Beat. Tick. Beat. Tick. Beat. Tick. My students sat with their backpacks in their hands. When the three p.m. bell rang, they bolted from the classroom. I waited a few minutes staring at the empty desks. A smile crossed my lips. Beat. Tick. Beat. Tick. Beat. Tick. The clock and I became friends again. I closed the classroom door and ran to the teacher's parking lot and my red BMW.

Greg called me on my cell phone when I was nearly home.

"Where the hell have you been?" I said. "You can't leave me in the lurch like this. I need you." I weaved through cars on the freeway and flashed my bright lights on the drivers who blocked my way to Greg.

"I've been tied up. Are you almost home?" Greg asked.

"Yeah."

"Good. I'm almost at your house. I'll let myself in."

I hung up, put the cell phone in my lap, and drove eighty-five miles an hour to get home to my lover Greg and the other lover he always brought for me.

⎯⎯⎯⎯◉⎯⎯⎯⎯

I PARKED MY CAR IN the back garage, slid past Greg's black BMW sedan, and entered through the kitchen door.

A pleasant fish aroma hit my nose, and I noticed the food bags from the seafood restaurant on the table. Jazz music played in the background. I dropped my purse and briefcase on the kitchen table.

"Greg, I'm here. I'm back."

Denise.

His cologne stirred my nose before I saw him. A grin crossed my face as he approached me. I stood in the hallway, and he greeted me with a kiss. His arms circled around my waist, and he pressed my body to his warm body. He stroked the jugular vein in my neck and rubbed my lips with his thumb.

"Every time you touch me, you take something from me, Greg," I whispered. "You weaken me — like you drain my life from me." I pulled his mouth to mine again, but he ended our kiss and pushed me away from him. He refused to look at me.

"Greg," I said pulling against his burgundy long-sleeved shirt. "Did you bring it?"

"I did, baby." He took my hands, pushed my sleeves up, and looked at my arms. "You keep this up, you won't be able to wear sleeveless dresses in the summer. You've got beautiful brown arms, baby."

I jerked my arms from him and pulled down my sleeves. "I don't have marks on my arms."

"Not yet you don't."

"Just give it to me all right." I held out my hand.

"No more shooting up."

He gave me a little coke in a pill container, and then we reheated seafood dinner in my microwave.

⎯⎯⎯⎯◉⎯⎯⎯⎯

GREG TOOK ME TO A PARTY of someone he called an associate. We entered the loft apartment in Downtown Dallas, which had three levels. So many people lived in downtown now that it resembled a city on television complete with men and women walking dogs on concrete streets and sidewalks to handle their daily business or to gain exercise. It no longer resembled the Downtown Dallas of my youth that contained shops galore and numerous food stands that served as my mall back in high school. Now it belonged to Dallas' elite crowd — young and old sophisticates — urban professionals with wealth. The techno music pounded in my chest. Leather sofas, hardwood floors, and African and Native American art hung on the walls.

Greg pushed a drink in my hand, and I gulped it down. My throat burned, but I didn't care. The only thing that mattered was being in Greg's presence. I sipped the second drink he gave me. Earlier Greg gave me a line of coke before we left for the party to loosen me up.

I smiled as we passed the beautiful people — the men and the women — and they were so beautiful they looked unnatural. It seemed as if someone had taken a magazine and blew breath on the images of the men and women hawking clothing, perfume, shoes, watches, rings, food and wished them to life. A hunger lingered in their eyes like the way Greg's eyes looked when he made love to me. Their hunger lingered in their eyes the same way a lion gazed at her prey on the African continent. Hungry. The hunter and the hunted. The longer they studied me, the weaker I felt. The hunger in their eyes surprised me. I saw that same hunger in Greg's eyes for me, as if he wanted more of me. Greg held my arm firmly when we passed the men, and the weakness passed.

"Denise, good to meet you," said one man who saluted me with his drink. "Greg's taking care of you?"

"Yes." I leaned into Greg, kissed him on the lips, and staggered a moment. "Greg takes care of me."

"She's your girl, Greg?"

"Yes, she is my girl." Greg nodded at the man who revealed an odd smile.

"The associates will remember."

A woman's scream surprised me. A crowd of partygoers ran to a circle of people. Greg grabbed my hand dragging me with him. In the center of the floor lay a woman, a beautiful woman, but her body danced on the floor. Her body jerked in odd angles. White foam covered her mouth. Her eyes rolled into the back of her head like a casino slot machine revealing only the whites of her eyes. My eyes widened, and I squeezed Greg's hand.

"Greg, they'll help her, right? She's not dying, right?"

Greg ignored my question and moved closer to the twitching woman.

"911's been called," a man said.

People scattered in the loft apartment. Toilets flushed, and sinks ran water. My drink fell from my hand and crashed onto the hardwood floor. I ignored the wetness on my black sheer thigh high stockings that Greg loved. "Greg, will 911 save her?"

Greg said nothing as he kneeled next to the woman. He placed his hands on her face and stomach, but the woman's twitching never stopped until the paramedics arrived taking the unmoving woman.

"Greg?" I raked my trembling fingers through my hair.

"She's becoming ... cold. Cold. She found her release, and now she's cold, Denise."

Greg stood next to me and took me in his arms. "You're warm, Denise," he whispered. "You're warm."

———◈———

I MISSED GREG WHEN he left town for two weeks for business, and I had no way to reach him, and he forgot to leave enough stuff to hold me over until his return. Sitting in class that Monday morning, I graded my students' history reports on the Vietnam War, and I was tired. I glanced repeatedly at the students as they read the next lesson in their history books and drummed my fingers on the wooden desk. I needed something now. I looked in my purse and didn't find any money. Leaving the classroom, I entered the hallway, strolled to the women's restroom, and pulled the fire alarm.

I hurried to my class, and frantic students left the classroom following Mrs. Jones, the math teacher. I told her I was sick and pointed to my stomach. The once quiet halls now buzzed with activity as teachers and students hurried outside. I closed my door and rifled through some of my students' backpacks. I retrieved a black laptop computer, and an electronic organizer from one backpack. From another, I found a twenty-dollar bill and a cell phone. Leaving the classroom door wide open, I placed the items in my red BMW trunk and left for the pawnshop.

———◉———

FRIDAY NIGHT I WAITED for Greg. I brushed my hair and ignored the clumps that fell in the sink. I used the bronze concealer to cover the dark circles under my eyes. The red makeup brightened my ashy skin. I hated my sunken cheeks, and my eyes looked too large protruding from my eye sockets. I covered my thinning hair with a black hat. My clothes hung on me like a starving supermodel.

Greg entered my house without knocking. He never knocked. He came into the living room and brought me food.

"Did you bring it? I need it again. You know how it is." I paced back and forth in front of Greg and hit my thighs with my fists. I took deep breaths. One. Breathe. Two. Breathe. One. Breathe. Two. Breathe.

"I brought you food to eat tonight, Denise." He remained sitting at the table wearing black slacks and a red pull over sweater.

"Yeah. That's nice. I need to be in a great mood for you, baby. Come on." I grabbed his hand and kissed it. "Do it for me, Greg. Take care of me."

Greg grabbed my arms and pushed the sweater's sleeves up. I tried removing my arms from him, but his strong grip held me. He studied my arms. "You've been shooting up again."

I didn't like his tone. He gave me a smoldering look, and his brown eyes darkened. He looked at street junkies and street whores like that. I'd seen him do it. "Greg, I couldn't wait for you. I needed something just one time and —"

"Damn it, Denise," he said walking away from me. "I told you not to get hooked to the heavy shit."

"But you gave it to me," I said tugging my hat tighter on my head.

"And you'd kill yourself if I told you to, right?"

"What are you talking about?" I sat on the coffee table and crossed my arms in front of my stomach. I rocked my body forwards and backwards. My hands twitched. "Greg, baby. I'm not so good right now. I'm not feeling well. Can you help me, baby? Let's not fight about this. Just this once. I'll stop."

Greg muttered something unintelligible under his breath. He left me sitting there on the coffee table rocking back and forth. The next minute I heard him cursing and slamming things around my bathroom. He cursed in English and in a language I didn't recognize.

I stopped rocking, crept down the hallway, and witnessed Greg cursing and tossing pills, powder, and glass vials down the toilet. He dumped my empty lipstick cases in the trash. He discarded my aspirin, my sinus medicine, my mouthwash, and my cold medicine with alcohol.

"What are you doing? Stop this!" I grabbed his arms, but he pushed me out of the bathroom. I leaned against the wall, sank to my knees, and watched Greg flush my lifeline down the toilet.

"I don't want to destroy you, Denise, not anymore," he said. "Your life is more than me, more than my need, more than you. You are meant for warm, not cold, Denise. I'm not giving you any more stuff. I'm not your supplier anymore."

I reached into my blue jeans pocket and pulled out crumpled bills. I threw the money at him. "I'll pay."

He looked at the four crumpled twenty-dollar bills and five ones that lay at his feet. Instead of taking my money, Greg stepped on the crumpled bills and scooped me up in his arms. I said nothing but allowed him to lead me. He grabbed the seafood bag in one hand and with his other arm around my shoulders led me to the garage.

He placed me in his black BMW and fastened the seat belt for me. I said nothing but stared straight ahead at the water hoses, hoes, spades, and shovels that hung in my garage. He got in the car and drove down the freeway. I watched his digital clock and found the beat tick beat tick beat tick missing. I closed my eyes, but the clock's light burned behind my lids. I gazed ahead at the road as we drove on Interstate 20. I only watched the lights on the eighteen-wheeler trucks as we traveled in rush hour traffic. The flashing lights of the sheriff's car caught my attention, and I hoped another officer would stop Greg from flying down the freeway and free me from his insanity because something is wrong with him. I closed my eyes again and heard Greg's voice fade in and out of my head.

"I can never go home again, Denise. I'm stuck here. I offered you the only gift that I could give — a release, allow you the pleasure of dying. I heard your thoughts and answered your call. In my home, pleasure and release from the pain was all that mattered. People suffered too much until we came. We were gods. We had a relationship with them. We gave them pleasure and a release and in return, we received longer life, strength, power, prestige, and wealth. I took the ones who wanted to die to their lives like you. Your anger for the man who left you at the altar destroys you."

My eyes flashed open and the blur of cars on the freeway agitated me more as I stared at him. "How do you know about that? Don't want to talk about it."

"But you do talk about it. The anger and the hurt have poisoned you to the point that you no longer care about living. It oozes from your pores even now," he paused. "If you were like me, you could smell it. I'm surprised none of the associates sensed your presence before me."

He paused looking at me, and I refused to meet his gaze. I concentrated on the blur then finding it too distracting closed my eyes and sighed. "You don't know what happened. I never told you about him," I mumbled remembering that stupid dress and invitations.

"True. You didn't tell me in the way you think. Your spirit did. You are the walking wounded like a hunted animal that is dying."

"Except I am not an animal. We are not animals."

He sighed. "The drugs never affected us the way they affected them. They weren't designed to match our chemical makeup. Something happened — I wanted a woman, and she wanted me. It drove me insane. I created an elixir except I didn't know what I did. I created something to bond a woman to me forever. She only wanted me and no one else."

"Drink. I want a drink."

Greg ignored me, and I hung my head down with my hands between my knees. My insides burned, I swallowed, and my dry mouth seemed bitter now remembering his kiss.

"I wasn't supposed to create a drug. I broke the law. The code. She became irrational. Dangerous. She only wanted me. I loved the power her wanting me gave me. I controlled her life, and she did everything, sacrificed everything for me. I killed her with my concoction, my creation. My team, my associates, told me to leave the city. They said my action drew too much attention to us. She was a high-profile woman hurting, and she called out to me. I answered her need. She died for me, but the authorities said I murdered her.

"They called us parasites. They sent us away — the ones who created this bond with men and women. I was sent here never to return to my home," Greg's voice paused again, and I heard him shift the gears. "No woman connected with me like she did in the way that I needed — until the day I saw the twitching woman from the party. I had given her something. She wanted to die too, except the child — I did not sense the growing life within her. I wouldn't have given it to her if I had known. She died on the floor at the party — one of mine, and I had no power to save her or save her child.

"I lost many of my gifts coming here, but I have connected to you in a way that gives me what I need," Greg said. "As I said Denise, you are meant for warm, not cold. I'm not giving you any more stuff. I'm not your supplier anymore."

I don't remember much of what Greg said. His voice bounced in my head as I slept, and I dreamed of distant cities, life in another land far away, white dresses, and I wanted the release and a forever bond.

<hr />

I MISSED DAYS FROM school, and Greg, controlling my life even more, decided a leave of absence was necessary and called the school. I'm not sure how he managed that feat. Greg barricaded me in his home or at least that's what it seemed to me. He never gave me keys to his place, and he took my red BMW keys and my purse away from me. He only left me with a driver's license. No one cleaned his home, which didn't even have a television. The beat tick beat tick beat tick of his grandfather clock in the hallway broke the home's silence. He fed me every day and locked the door.

Greg left me, and I hated being in his home alone. I picked up his phone and found it dead. I slammed the phone on the receiver and peered out the window. Raising the bedroom window and removing the screen, I escaped Greg's home after being there for seven days.

I walked downtown. A couple of hookers offered their services to me, but I ignored them. I passed the street people, and the winos shoved their brown bags of liquor in my face. BMWs, Volvos, Vipers, Mercedes, and other expensive cars cruised the strip. A few men called to me asking for conversation, but I searched for the man who could save me. That man found me first. The man approached me wearing his brown leather jacket and expensive matching shoes.

"You look like you need a friend."

"I do."

"What do you want to work out?"

"Can we talk about this at my home?"

He put his arm around me, and I smiled for the first time that night.

A few minutes later in Greg's living room, I negotiated with the man for some of his best stuff. I didn't offer him money, but I kneeled on my knees — his discount since I was a first-time customer.

I unzipped the man's pants, heard his intake of breath, looked up at him, and saw his widened eyes. Muffled footsteps on carpet behind us interrupted me.

Greg's hand landed on my shoulder pushing me to the floor. I scooted away from him on my butt, and he grabbed the seated man from the couch.

"Greg, I didn't know it was your house!" the man screamed. "I didn't know she was your girl. No one told me."

Greg threw the man to the couch, pulled a gun from his black jacket, and pointed the gun at the man's chest. Where had Greg purchased the gun? I had never seen it before. I stared at Greg and the man and scooted further away from them.

"Rico, now you know," Greg pointed the gun at Rico's chest. "This one is to be untouched. I've claimed her for myself. The connection has been established between us."

"I'll tell the associates. We all don't go the parties, Greg. It's an honest mistake."

"If you honed your senses you would have known she was taken. She has my scent, my stamp now. Did you touch her?"

"No. Nothing happened."

"No bond?"

"No."

Greg sighed and lowered the gun from the man named Rico's chest. Rico glanced at me, but I averted my eyes as he zipped his pants. Greg nodded his head towards the door, and Rico, my almost lover, left the apartment. Greg stared at the door with the gun still in his hand like a child holding a broken toy, except I knew that his toy, his gun, worked.

Seeking escape, I crawled on my hands and my knees to my room, but Greg blocked my path. He yanked me by the arms from the floor, but I refused to look at him. Instead, I stared at his black leather shoes.

"Was that the way you were going to pay him?"

"You took my money," I said.

"I'm trying to help you."

"Give me the stuff then take it away, huh? Some help you are. I don't need this."

I stormed past him, but he grabbed my chin and forced me to look at him. "I need you to live, Denise."

"Why do you care so much?" I said.

He removed his hand and walked away from me.

———— ◉ ————

THE NEXT FRIDAY, GREG found me on the bathroom floor.

"Denise! Denise!"

He screams my name, but he sounds so far away. His body floats in slow motion as his hand reaches for the cordless phone. He returns to my side and calls someone, I think. His lips move, but I hear no words. I feel like a swimmer underwater surrounded by red, white, and purple lights and silence. I try focusing on Greg, but my eyes refuse to stay open. I try lifting my arm, but it remains on the floor. I look at Greg and see the red, white, and purple lights again. Music bounces in my head, and my body twitches like a mechanical toy.

"Purple," I mumble and close my eyes again.

Men wearing blue rolling a bed lift me in their warm arms, and I snuggle closer to the man's chest. He pushes me away and the cold, the cold, the cold, and the water, and the water, and the water... popping of my ears. Yes, close my eyes and the purple surrounds me like a lover, and I reach out to that lover, and he takes me never letting me go, and I smile, I think. Greg's so kind. He plays my colors, my song, my music, for me because he loves me...like the puppy licking my face now... he takes the puppy away ...and it whimpers ... the water covers me like a mother's womb, and I've returned home.

Why do they want me to leave this place? Yes, the cold leaves me I think, and I snuggle deeper into the sea of purple, my water for me. I look up and see strange bottles and shiny metal and yellow. Greg sits there above me away from the water. I try to reach him, but my hands won't obey me. Won't he join me in this place? The place he told me about it...so happy ...free... purple ...wait a minute. What... are they... doing? The men jostle me on the table taking me away from the water, the cold. No...give it back to me...leave me with my lover...don't you see...Greg won't mind...ambulance rushes me to the emergency room ... and doctors and nurses and technicians laugh at me as they pull my clothes from my body...their machines the beeps the flashing lights...ouch the tape...pulls the hair on my arm ...the needle pricks my arm...smile yes...they want me to have fun with my lover again...yes I can't wait to see the purple...won't Greg take me to that place again...the lights and the purple and the beat tick beat tick beat tick...match my heart...pump me don't you want to pump me, Greg.

I smile and their hands punch my stomach pinch my cheeks...the doctor...lifts my lid shines tiny white dot in my eye.... hey...not purple...I like purple... pump my stomach. I see Greg's shadow ... the doctor's blue scrubs ... back and forth ... match the red, white, and purple lights. I cough. They cover my mouth and nose. I take deep breaths. One. Breathe. Two. Breathe. One. Breathe. I float on the air in the pretty lights.

———◦———

LATER I WOKE UP NOT floating on air, but I found myself in a bed. My throat burned. Opening my eyes, I noticed a red-eyed Greg sitting at my bedside. He grabbed my hands and kissed them. He ignored the tubes that ran the length of my arms, and his warm hands and hot tears covered my hands.

"Denise, Denise," he mumbled. "You really wanted to die. If you died, you would have been the third woman." Sobs wracked his body.

I opened my mouth, but no sound left my lips. I heard the beeping monitor and smiled. Beat. Tick. Beat. Tick. Beat. Tick. The sound matched my heart.

———◦———

TWELVE MONTHS HAVE passed since I found myself drowning in purple. I remember it now like the remnants of a dream that haunt the soul years after when one wonders what the symbols mean. I remember purple, lights, and water. Feeling brave enough, I find a compelling desire to revisit the scene of my downfall like some criminal who returns to his crime to admire his handiwork. Greg takes me to the nightclub, but insists we restart and give our relationship a new beginning.

I dressed in a red sleeveless gown that revealed smooth brown arms. I'd cut my hair off since it became so thin and wore a small Afro.

Walking onto the middle of the dance floor, I moved my feet and shoulders from right to left and offered my hand to Greg — the god-man I met at the club who told me I wanted to die. The flashing red, white, and purple lights shined on our faces as we embraced. The black-and-white strobe light slowed our movements. I tilted my head to look up at him, and his chest felt warm against my skin.

"You called me," he said.

I spun around and waved my bare brown arms in the air to the music.

Beat. Tick. Beat. Tick. Beat. Tick. I took his hand in mine.

Nirvana

Deron watched the bleeding man crumple in the alley before him among the trash and old soiled cardboard boxes. The man clutched at his stomach with both hands and looked up at Deron who towered above him in the night-filled alley. Rain fell on the man's hands and on his face, but he continued staring up at Deron. Deron watched the man's hands clutch at his stomach, but the rain mingled with his red blood creating a pink hue. The man coughed and wheezed, and more red life flowed between his fingers.

Placing his handgun back into his jacket, Deron glanced to the left and right in the alley , kneeled next to the man, retrieved the man's bag once his own, and took out a silver pocketknife, and sliced the black cross on plastic string from around the man's neck. The man wheezed and clutched at his stomach again as he lay among the trash. Deron stood up again and blocked the stars from the man's eyes.

"You don't steal from me," he said. "You forgot who you were dealing with, old man."

"Curse you, Deron," the man yelled as the strength left his body.

Deron walked away from the man whose wheezing and breathing became shallower until he died. He heard the man's last breath as his boots echoed in the alley and the dark puddles of water. The rain stopped.

Deron's life changed tonight with his escape plan from District 933. He tied the cross around his neck and placed it under his shirt and walked down the dark alley. He pulled his jacket tighter. Despite the chill, sweat rolled down from his armpits. He glanced around making sure no one followed him.

He heard a cat howl and saw it skitter before him to a trash heap. The scrawny, ruffled animal would have a short life if it remained careless. Some hungry wretch would catch the cat making it a prime stew ingredient for the community. His lips curled in disgust. He hated eating cats, dogs, old breads, or sickly vegetables. He hated eating nothing, but his luck would change when he found the Informer. He walked harder. He turned another corner and crept down another alley.

The Informer.

No one knew much about him except that he came to you.

Last month, Deron stood in a soup line when he felt a warm sensation spread across his back. He turned around and noticed a man standing near a pole. Deron's olive-green eyes narrowed with suspicion as he studied the man. The man wore a long, black overcoat. A black, wool fedora covered his head. Dark shades concealed the man's eyes although it was late evening. Even among the misfits and miscreants of District 933, he seemed an oddity. Deron stroked his black goatee as he stared at the man. He knew this man.

The Informer watched Deron.

When the Informer walked the streets, people cleared the sidewalks. Residents offered their soup or bread to him. Women smiled offering him comforts for a night.

The Informer never said a word to anyone, but everyone knew he represented the way to freedom. Rumors said he escaped District 933 many years ago, but he returned to help others escape. No one sought the Informer out for a means of an escape. He made the choice. He offered a new life for one individual each time. All prayed he would offer them the chance.

As Deron stared at the Informer, he knew he wanted to escape District 933 — the district designated for the undesirables and their descendants. No one called Dallas City by its true name anymore after the Bad Times of 2015 nearly two hundred years ago. Instead, the city had been divided into districts to protect residents, but everyone knew the Enforcers, the police force, designed the system to keep them caged up in their district. Shortly after the Bad Times, the thirteen-foot concrete wall came up separating the districts forever. Time passed and a new history filtered down to the District 933 descendants. No one really remembered life before 2015, and the stories residents heard made good tales around trash barrels of fire.

However, Deron studied the stories and knew that with most tales told by old men there existed some truth no matter how diluted with exaggeration. And that's why he chose to leave District 933. He hated the filth, the smell, the hopelessness. He desired more, and those who lived in Nirvana Province owed him.

He had no desire to work the mines until he succumbed to old age or a cave-in. How long had he worked the mines? He remembered little about his first day except that two Enforcers grabbed him and pressed his hands into the scanner. The red light cast an eerie glow on his ebony skin. Now they had his identity forever. He hated that they could track him. The microbes would remain forever embedded underneath his skin. And for what? Those who lived in District 933 slaved for the comfort of those who lived in Nirvana Province. Everyone knew the truth, but few dared to speak it aloud. Residents said Enforcers walked in their midst, but Deron never expressed his political ideas. He stared at the Informer and walked away from the soup line.

As he approached the man, he swallowed. What would he say to the Informer? Would he express his gratitude at being chosen? No, Deron had to be a soldier. He calmed his breathing and stood taller. It was an honor to be worthy of the Informer's time.

"Soldier, are you ready?" He said brisk, business-like.

Deron blinked with surprise. What had he expected? A rallying cry from a general to his troops before entering battle? "Yes, Informer. I am ready."

The Informer looked past Deron at the soup line. "The way will not be easy."

"I am ready."

"It will be dangerous."

"I am a brave man. I fear nothing," said Deron with an edge of impatience creeping into his voice.

"There are those who would kill you without a thought."

"And I would kill them before they kill me. They deserve to die for what they have done to us," Deron snapped.

The Informer snatched off his shades and glared at him. Deron gasped. The Informer's lips contorted on his albino face. The man's raven eyes pierced Deron's soul, and he felt a burning sensation. His chest tightened. Coldness spread into Deron's fingertips.

"Young fool! That lust for vengeance will get you killed!" The Informer stammered with rage. "Perhaps some deserve to die, but it is not for you to decide that."

Deron said nothing but dropped his head for a moment. His black shoulder-length dreadlocks dangled in his face. He watched his hands clasp and unclasp again. When he lifted his head, he saw the Informer walking away.

"Informer, wait. I apologize for my anger. I am ready," Deron said struggling to control his quavering voice.

The Informer stopped and faced him. Again, the dark shades covered his eyes. "You are not ready." Without another word, the Informer continued walking into the darkness.

Deron stood there feeling the eyes of the soup line behind him. They witnessed it all — his acceptance and rejection by the Informer. He heard their whispers and felt his face grow hot. He balled his fists. He would find the Informer again. And he would escape District 933 to live forever in Nirvana Province.

The Informer's rejection of Deron had been a month ago and no matter how hard Deron searched, the Informer eluded him. But he would find him tonight.

Deron lurked down another darkened alley. After he turned the last corner, he felt a presence. Someone followed him. He turned around and saw nothing. He pressed his back against the brick wall and grabbed the gun in his pocket.

"Deron, I hear you've been looking for me."

Deron aimed the gun at the Informer who stood in a doorway. He lowered his weapon. The Informer's raven eyes glinted in the moonlight. The man's albino face resembled marble.

"Curb your anger, Deron. My life is my own affair," he said crisply as he walked down the steps of the doorway. "But you want a new life."

"You knew I was searching for you."

"If you were weak, you would have remained standing in the soup lines forever. I knew your heart had courage. Your persistence showed me that you were ready for freedom. You passed the test, but enough time has wasted. Come. It is time to complete your training."

Deron followed him down the darkened alley.

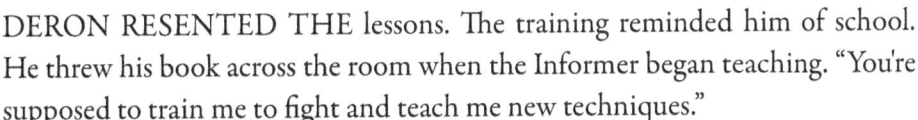

DERON RESENTED THE lessons. The training reminded him of school. He threw his book across the room when the Informer began teaching. "You're supposed to train me to fight and teach me new techniques."

"Why should I, Deron? You already know how to kill. I cannot perfect the art of killing another human being. I teach you how to live." He stared at the book in the floor then walked closer to Deron. "When you cross The Wall, you must act, think, and believe that you belong there without question! Your arrogance and anger make you hold your head high, and this defiance burns in your soul. Even now you want to strike me."

"Informer, I respect you for who you are and what you represent. Nothing more." Deron retrieved his book from the floor. "Continue the lesson."

———◉———

DERON PRESSED THE BINOCULARS closer to his face as he watched the old school bus leave District 933 for the mines. The bus had once been bright yellow, but time and neglect changed its appearance. Enforcers stood near the bus with rifles slung over their shoulders and handguns at their waists as the miners prepared for their day of drudgery.

Since his training with the Informer, Deron no longer worked the mines. The residents of District 933 never saw Deron again, and the appearance of a severely burned body identified as Deron confirmed him as a casualty. Once the body appeared, the Enforcers ended their interrogation of the residents about Deron's whereabouts. They cared little for the lives of the District 933 residents or the crimes they inflicted upon each other. But if a District 933 resident committed an offense against an Enforcer, punishment came swiftly. Someone died to send a message.

At the end of each day, the workers spilled from the bus tired, dirty, and angry. Many who had water went to their own homes and dwellings they shared with others to rid themselves of the grit and smell. The ones who had no place to call their own stood in the soup line waiting for food and water to cleanse themselves.

Life existed that way in District 933 as far as Deron could recall. Old, abandoned cars rusted from years of neglect often served as homes for some less fortunate. People walked or ran in District 933. No one had gas to power a vehicle and even if anyone did, no one believed that the car would even move except the Informer who taught Deron to drive his old jeep. The Informer never explained how he acquired the jeep or how he fueled it.

In fact, the Informer told Deron that long ago life had been different in District 933. Once there had been no walls separating them from the other district, but those times existed before the Informer's birth.

Deron gave a mocking laugh. "You lie, Informer. You sound like the old men who tell ghost stories. If these people lived as such, they would not have allowed this to happen."

The Informer said nothing but stared at Deron as they walked across the dusty plains leading to the grove of dead trees that grew near The Wall.

"Have you ever looked over The Wall?"

"Everyone knows you'll be shot if you dare or electrocuted by the energy field near The Wall."

"And yet, you were never curious? It can be disabled."

"Yes, I want to know what's on the other side. I'm not an animal that they can keep caged and locked up forever."

"Would you kill any of them if you got over on the other side?"

Deron smirked saying nothing. They returned to his training. The lesson had ended for the day.

———◉———

TWO MONTHS LATER, DERON stood near the tunnel's entrance in Old City where no one lived anymore. Residents said chemicals from a long ago lead smelter polluted the area. To enter Old City was to bring death much faster. Rumor or truth had kept people away from freedom, Deron thought. He pressed his lips together as he twisted his dreadlocks into one braid down his back.

Deron wiped the sweat from his face as he hid in the brush and tangled dead trees, which grew thick. He cursed under his breath. The Informer said a grove of trees existed near the old tunnel's entrance outside the main city limits, but not those with prickly thorns. His skin burned with scratches from thorns and branches, but he would escape District 933 and live in Nirvana Province forever. He looked in the night sky for the patrol helicopter's search light. The sky rumbled; it would rain soon.

The half-moon illuminated the surroundings occasionally only to be concealed by the dark clouds and rising wind. As he watched the half-moon,

Deron remembered the Informer's lessons. During his training, he lived, slept, and bathed in the Informer's dwelling. The Informer talked about the habits of the Nirvana Province residents. He explained the strange wonders that would greet his eyes. He told him how to get a job and gave him money to purchase goods and a home. He indoctrinated him until Deron believed that he belonged in Nirvana Province as his natural birthright. He listened in awe as the man explained how to live, but Deron's impatience tried the Informer during their sessions. Yet, the Informer's cold logic and raven eyes silenced Deron's outbursts.

The Informer stood next to him in the brush as both surveyed the map again for the tenth time in the last two weeks.

"After all this time, you don't think I'm ready do you, Informer?"

The Informer watched him silently.

"But I am ready, and I'll prove you wrong and all the others."

The Informer reached into his pocket and handed Deron a wallet. With his other hand, he handed him a huge canvas bag.

"Everything you need is in the bag. Soldier, so that your soul will live free and you escape eternal damnation, help the rest of District 933. Be wise and trust no one. Be alert. You fight for your right to live when you cross The Wall to Nirvana Province," he said. "Remember this, Deron. Conceal your coming and going so only the moon knows. Conceal your heart so that only God knows, but do His will."

"What? A riddle? How is a damn riddle going to help me leave this stinking rat hole?" Deron asked.

"The riddle may save your life and your soul, soldier." The Informer turned and walked away through the grove of dead trees and brush.

As Deron watched the Informer disappear through the grove of dead trees and brush, he wondered how many District 933 residents had escaped and lived?

DERON CALMED HIS BREATHING. He neared The Wall, which separated him from freedom. He would make it to the other side. He jumped inside and landed in what looked like an abandoned drain system. His flashlight illuminated the drainpipe revealing gray walls. Soiled newspaper and other litter covered the tunnel's floor. He walked for several feet before coming to the end, which ended with a huge metal door. He beat against the metal door before it gave way to another tunnel leading upward. Deron climbed up the tunnel's ladder. He pushed against the final door and peered around before lifting it further.

Deron emerged in what looked like a garbage dump park. Darkness hung in the air. He walked through the dump toward the rising sun.

<hr>

THE SUN'S WARMTH AND intensity in Nirvana Province surprised Deron. Its brilliance compared to nothing like the pale disc he knew as the sun. Thick fog covered his sun, or perhaps it refused to shine in District 933.

He stared at every building. Clear glass windows without metal bars reflected his image back to him. Red brick accented the buildings. Smooth, unbroken steps led to clothing and jewelry stores. The grocery stores offered fresh fruit for picking. Music and laughter filled his ears. People walked the streets with their children for Saturday shopping, the Informer called it. Their arms carried bags filled with boxes of clothing and bags of food. Everyone smiled in Nirvana Province. Their faces glowed in the bright sun. A floral scent hung in the air, and Deron inhaled. The scented water of the men and women intoxicated him. A woman passed by, and he wanted to hold her close to drink in the scent again. The Informer warned him of the arousing nature of the colognes and perfumes. He ignored the sensations.

Deron remembered the smell of trash soups, which consisted of old vegetables and catch of the day. The servers offered hard bread with the soup. Residents of his district only ate from trash soups when they contributed something. Some days he had nothing to contribute, which meant tightening his belt or standing in the soup line.

"Young man? Young man?"

Deron stopped walking and stared at the old woman dressed in white. "Yes?" He balled his fists.

"Young man, take some of my soup of the day. It's free. Come back to our hotel later for the festival and eat more."

Deron took the miniature paper bowl and plastic spoon. The brown soup had chunks of meat and vegetables. He swallowed, and the spicy taste made him stagger. He ate it in her presence. "What do you call it?"

"Mabel's Gumbo."

She gave him another bowl, and he continued his trek through the streets of Nirvana Province. Deron stared at the paved streets of Nirvana Province with awe. The streets looked clean enough for sleeping, Deron thought. This place, Nirvana Province, was the district of dreams. It was unlike his district, which screamed songs of chaos and despair. Unpaved streets covered his district, and the rains flooded the deep holes in the street. In his homeland, music never greeted his ears with warm welcome. Instead, children beat on tin cans and blew crudely fashioned whistles or flutes. No stores enticed District 933 residents with their wares. Abandoned buildings of what may have been two hundred years ago covered his homeland. Did anyone ever smile? He couldn't remember. He only saw anger and sadness reflected from their faces.

What joy did District 933s have? Was it only in sex? When their bodies threw all despairing thoughts to the wind just to be pulsing, sweating bodies? And for a moment, the horrors of District 933 seemed far away maybe even a bad dream. But after the high, when the euphoria faded, reality crushed them. People ran from their temporary bliss to hide in their cubbyholes until the next time the desire to forget was stronger than contempt for their existence.

Deron caught the bus. He had no idea where he traveled, but he wanted to see all of Nirvana Province. When he stepped on the bus, the first thing he noticed was the driver's friendly greeting. The man offered him donuts and juice. He thanked him and took a back seat near a window. He wolfed down the donuts and gulped the juice. He glimpsed at the remaining donuts and juice but refrained from asking for more.

He sighed. How could life be so tragically different in one city divided by The Wall and a district? Deron nestled into the blue, crushed velvet seats. His lids grew heavy. He couldn't remember sleeping in such comfort. After he lost his fine dwelling, he slept in an abandoned building on a floor he shared with other residents, roaches, and rats.

Deron dreamed.

THE JOLT OF THE BUS stopping woke Deron from his slumber. He looked at the park and saw children playing. He pressed his face closer to the window. These children with clean faces and clothes laughed. Deron knew why the children laughed as they played. They never went hungry. Their full cheeks told him as much. Their parents stayed with them while District 933 children's parents worked the mines. Deron lowered his head. He now knew the children never received the money for their parents' labors. He never knew his parents. He learned his education from the older women of District 933 who took it upon themselves to teach the youths.

After passing the children, Deron left the bus. Anger filled him as he walked through the neighborhood of huge homes, clean sidewalks, and manicured green lawns. He blinked as he stared at the lawns. Paper, broken glass and concrete slabs cluttered District 933. If grass grew in abundance in District 933, it had long ceased its growth. The sun refused to shine across The Wall in District 933 it seemed. Even the sun gave up on the badlands, as the mine guards called it. He lived on barren wasteland, and they expected him to make a living.

Once the barren wasteland yielded a patch of fertile soil bringing forth tiny buds. Then Deron and a friend tended the garden and shared its spoils. The two of them relished their garden until the day they found the older boys stealing their prized vegetables. His eyes blazed with anger as he charged the biggest boy.

The boy grabbed him by his dreadlocks jerking his head back. "You want to fight me, you little insignificant? You want to fight me?"

Deron kicked the boy in the groin and immediately felt the boy's wrath as his fists pounded him. He cried out and saw the other boys beat his friend.

When he opened his eyes, the sky looked red. Wiping the blood from his forehead, he limped to the still form of his friend. His neck lay at a strange angle. Deron cried. His frail, boyish body heaved with sobs. He didn't care if the big boys saw him or came back. They killed his best friend. The big boys destroyed their garden and stole their food.

"Remember this day and live, boy."

Deron peered about wild-eyed for the owner of the voice, but no one materialized. An adult had witnessed it all.

Deron had been ten years old, but twenty years later the memory haunted him still. He pressed his lips together firmly and popped his knuckles as he continued walking in the Nirvana Province neighborhood. The darkness covered his face again, and Deron remembered the revenge he meted against the boys. He met them in the mines, older and crueler, but so was he. He killed them all but not before he revealed his identity to them and their crime.

The Enforcers locked him in solitary confinement for his actions, but Deron didn't care. He destroyed the men who killed the only thing he had enjoyed in District 933 – his best friend. They took away his innocence that day in the garden. He never returned.

So engrossed was Deron in his thoughts that he stumbled. Fuming he looked down and noticed a piece of wood. Upon closer inspection, Deron found the wood to be a hoe nearly buried in grass. He had stopped outside of a beautiful, brick home. Unlike the other lawns, the grass stood tall. He stared at the iron gate when he noticed the sign. Gardener wanted. A cunning grin crossed Deron's face. He had a job.

———◉———

THREE MONTHS HAD PASSED, and Deron enjoyed working for the old woman. Her husband could no longer maintain the enormous lawn. Deron thought this an easy task. His payment consisted of a cottage in back and meals, and she wanted him to be a driver. She gave him free use of the jeep, but not the red sports car. He laughed when she explained that her husband bought the contraption to recapture his lost youth.

He would never use it again. The old man said nothing as he sat in his wheelchair. He only gave Deron a blank stare. A stroke ravaged his body a year before leaving him nothing but a shell of a man.

———◉———

ONE DAY THE OLD WOMAN ran to the back lawn in her pink robe and matching slippers. A frantic look crossed her face. Deron knew something had happened to the old man. He stopped trimming the bushes and waited until she reached him.

"Good heavens, Deron! The vandals will pillage everything. We must protect ourselves."

Deron raised an eyebrow. "Vandals, Mrs. O?" He mispronounced her name, so she insisted that he call her Mrs. O.

"Deron, the Enforcers say the other ones … the ones who live," she glanced behind her and stepped closer to him. Her small blue eyes seemed hidden in her lined face. "The ones who live in District 933 have found a way into our city … a tunnel," she whispered.

Deron's eyes widened in alarm. He gripped the hoe tighter as he listened to Mrs. O. He felt the small hairs on the back of his neck stir. He calmed his breathing to steady the pounding of his heart, which thundered in his ears.

"The Enforcers say they are … cannibals and heathens. They have no morality. They kill themselves. May the Enforcers catch them and shoot them dead. Simply dreadful, Deron. Dreadful, I tell you." She returned to the house muttering to herself. When she reached the glass doorway, she yelled. "Deron, lock the gates every night. We can't let one of those fiends in here."

"Yes, Mrs. O. We can't let one of those fiends in here."

<hr />

DERON PACED IN HIS cottage. He ran his hands through his shoulder-length dreadlocks and cursed. Mrs. O had called it small, but in fact, the four-room cottage could house twenty people in District 933. Fool. The Enforcers had found the tunnel. What other evidence had they found? The old woman's tart lemonade, which he had acquired a taste for, remained untouched this evening. If the Enforcers discovered him, his new life would end. He shuddered.

Deron opened his duffel bag, which he had hidden underneath the wooden floorboards and retrieved his gun. It was time to carry his one true friend again. It would never fail. He had no time to worry about the Informer's riddle, but unwanted, the riddle sang loudly in his head.

Conceal your coming and going so only the moon knows. Conceal your heart so that only God knows, but do His will.

Deron fell asleep holding his gun.

DERON WOKE IN A COLD sweat staring at the ceiling. He left the tunnel exposed to the Enforcers who patrolled the border. How could he have known that the trash dump would be searched? In his excitement, he failed to cover the tunnel. Damn. And he remembered the last words of the Informer. Helping those who remained behind in District 933 was the only way he would escape eternal damnation. Deron damned himself as far as he was concerned. He committed acts to extend his life over other District 933 residents.

He stole food to feed his hunger.

He killed a man for his boots.

He even killed a child — his own.

He knew she was pregnant and wondered how long she would wait to tell him. Before the child's appearance, life in District 933 had been bearable because of Cynthia's love for him. He smiled then, but he had a different life with a contact who smuggled goods from Nirvana Province into District 933. He had fine clothes, fine food, and a fine dwelling. Their lifestyle changed when someone killed his contact. Later, the child's appearance added to his anger and reminded him of their dwindling food.

She tried to hide her condition from him by changing in the dark and away from his eyes, but she forgot that she slept in his bed every night. He knew every curve, every hair, every scar, and every blemish. His hands knew Cynthia's body in the dark, his hands knew Cynthia's body in the water, and his hands knew Cynthia's body in the light. Because he knew Cynthia's body, he watched the changes in her body with interest — the swelling of her breasts, the swelling of her hips, and the swelling of her stomach. She could no longer hide from him. He knew she carried an insignificant thing inside of her, and he wanted no part of it.

He ordered Cynthia to have an abortion. His reasoning seemed logical. Spare a child the horrors of District 933. Liar. His sentiments sounded noble, but harsh to Cynthia who carried his spawn. He had no desire to see a filthy child walking around with his eyes staring at him begging for food. The thought of a little insignificant child with his eyes appalled him. Soldiers had no time for ties.

Cynthia hid herself from him in the old theater's film projector room. Three days later he found her sleeping on the floor covered with a blanket, and two of his associates grabbed her. She had uttered declarations of love for him as he injected her arm with the medication to make her sleep.

He left her in the back door clinic that handled these matters. He waited in the recovery room and heard her screams, her sobs, and her silence. When the butcher came demanding payment, Deron handed over a coat, shoes, and food.

"Will she live?"

The man nodded as he put on his new coat.

Deron left the back door clinic and Cynthia alone. He never saw her again.

Did the Informer believe hope existed for him yet? He stared at the canned food he had hoarded for six months.

DERON TRAVELED THE paved road to District 933. The paved road ended, and he drove the jeep across the dirt road. As he neared The Wall, he fidgeted in his seat. He wiped his clammy palms on his jeans. He never thought he would return to District 933 let alone escape it.

The sky darkened and he heard thunder. Strange. It reminded him of the night he left District 933. He clutched the wheel and drove faster. Once he neared the Old City border, he dropped the boxes of food over The Wall. The Informer would retrieve the food.

Deron glanced at the violet sky. The sun would rise soon, and the patrols would come. Deron returned to the jeep when he heard the low growl of a dog. He stiffened when the lights flashed on him, but he tried to relax. He covered his eyes with his hands.

"Who's there? Hello? Who's there?" he asked.

Before hearing a reply, the sound of swift feet thundered in his ears. The dog leaped knocking him to the ground. Someone grabbed the dog, and then a man's gruff voice spoke.

"Citizen, you're under arrest."

"On what grounds?" Deron muttered as another man attached metal cuffs to his wrists.

"For being a District 933 sympathizer."

THE BRIGHT LIGHT BLINDED Deron in the Enforcers' interrogation room. Their faces remained hidden in shadow, but from their muttering, he knew they had found his belongings and other items linking him to District 933. He relaxed a moment then stiffened. He glanced at his hands then lowered them. How could he have forgotten the scanned handprints? The Enforcers scanned all residents of District 933 who worked the mines. The tiny microbes embedded in his skin confirmed his true identity. He caught snatches of their muffled voices and heard fingerprints and District 933 clearly.

They knew Deron. They knew he lived beyond The Wall.

"What's your number?"

Deron remained silent in the cold, sterile room. He heard several voices around him. He watched the Inquisitor walk around him before the man's fist landed in his jaw.

"Perhaps you didn't hear me. What's your number?"

"My name is Deron," he said as he spit the blood from his mouth. To his dismay, the Inquisitor hit him again and pushed him onto the floor. Deron spit blood from his mouth again and panted as the Inquisitor circled closer around him. In a swift movement, Deron leaped, grabbed the man, and twisted his neck. The Inquisitor fell to the ground.

The remaining Enforcers surrounded Deron in outrage and kicked him. Their kicks tore at his body. He would die here beneath their boots. How many had they killed from District 933? The kicks ceased and Deron groaned in the floor. One Enforcer sat him in the chair again and handcuffed his hands behind his back.

"Like the Inquisitor said, 'what's your number?' This time if you try something foolish, I will kill you," he paused. "What's your number?"

"I will die before I tell you," he sneered. Deron kicked the man in his groin. He doubled over with pain and Deron smirked, but his victory was short-lived. Another Enforcer's fist hit his jaw except this time the man wore several rings. Deron closed his mouth ignoring the pain in his jaw. He grimaced.

"I have a name. I am Deron from District 933," he said through clenched teeth. "You keep us away because you fear us, but I live again thanks to one who saw darkness in my soul." He gave the silhouetted guards around him a scorched look. "Live as I lived and face eternal damnation, Enforcers," Deron cried.

"Did you think you could make it, live here in Nirvana Province? Did you really believe that you'd be allowed to go about your leave?" asked the Enforcer as he circled Deron. "Your kind isn't wanted around here. You know the law."

"Your law is nothing!"

"Your genetically flawed ways would corrupt us all. You are greedy. You prey on each other like animals. You kill. You steal. No, you are a liability and that's why you remain in District 933. That's why you work the mines."

"If we are flawed, it is because you allowed us to be treated like animals who live to survive," Deron said. "Something has gone horribly wrong. The ones who came before us didn't mean for this life to be so.

"Where is it written that a man cannot rise and dream of a better life for himself or his family? Who are you to tell anyone or me from District 933 that we and our descendants must remain and forever work in your mines? It is not we who are flawed, Enforcer. It is you. You have condemned an entire people out of fear."

"No one from District 933 is allowed here ever," the Enforcer said. "That is the law that I uphold and believe. You are nothing but a liability to us."

"You have condemned me because I come from District 933. In your eyes, I'm no more than your slave. I'm human just like you, but that doesn't matter to you," Deron said. He glared at the darkness. Every draw of breath caused him pain. His ribs ached, and he knew they were broken. "The day will come when you pay for what you've done. I'll have my revenge," he said.

The Enforcers stood quietly in the room. The second Inquisitor broke the stillness.

"Kill him."

The boots battered Deron again, and he blacked out into darkness. He smiled when he saw Cynthia's face in the darkness. "Forgive me, Cynthia. I have wronged you," he said but his lips made no sound in the darkness, and Cynthia's image faded.

THE INFORMER WATCHED the Enforcer patrol dump the body. It remained on the ground for hours. No one came to retrieve it. No one came to prepare it for burial. No one came because no one knew it was there.

He walked to The Wall and shook his head. He carried the boxes of food to his jeep then looked at the dividing wall again. The Informer looked at the cloudy sky and buttoned his coat. He pulled the wool fedora closer to his head and stuffed his hands in his pockets. His record needed cleaning. Another mistake. Would he ever find others to stay long enough to liberate the people of District 933?

Deron had lived longer than most — six months in Nirvana Province. Other recruits had been killed once they arrived. Some failed to contain their excitement of being in Nirvana Province without a barbed wire and a stone wall surrounding them drawing attention. Many escaped their prison, but no one survived long enough to tell or help anyone except him.

He escaped first from District 933 and survived in Nirvana Province. He lived in the beautiful district for fifteen years but returned to help his people. No one knew the truth. The brittle grass and brush crunched under his feet as he picked up Deron's broken body. He placed Deron in the jeep and drove back to District 933.

Ring

After spending time with Deron for nearly a year, I wanted to bond our union. I wanted to bond myself to Deron — to the warmth of his body, the laughter of his mouth, the breath of his lungs, the manhood of his body, the desire of his body for my body, and the spark in his brown eyes. I took my extra food cans, a lock of my hair, and went to the metal works man. He took what I had, and he made me the ring.

"It's not true gold. It will turn, Cynthia."

"I don't care," I said flashing the gold-colored band in the firelight. "It's perfect."

"It's not perfect. Nothing ever is," the man said.

"You sound like the Informer."

The metal works man grunted and stroked the roaring fire with his metal stick.

The Informer seems more a myth than a man with his escape from District 933, our prison, nearly twenty years ago. He blinded his captors with his raven eyes and snow-white skin. His mouth uttered curses that stilled the hearts of his captors, and his arms crushed the life from his captors, so the stories said with each retelling. After his escape, he lived in the free District of 934 called Nirvana Province. However, he'd returned to our prison to help us since things remained desolate after the Fourth War ended sixty years ago. The country had been divided up into new districts, and military officials relocated people to this district.

The limited history of this district I know is from what people have told me. I know that we aren't allowed to leave it. The Wall running around the district separates us from Nirvana Province, the place we've heard about all our lives. Residents here call that place paradise, a place where the sun shines warming the skin where children smile and where adult laughter fills the streets and people live in cities where food and water are plentiful. There are no soup lines there. Small families live in dwellings that can house at least twenty

District 933 residents, each with their own rooms. No one works the mines in that place; they have jobs and careers.

I've heard old ones here say that one hundred fifty years ago things were different. I've seen relics from those past days — televisions that no longer work, rusted cars that people sleep or have sex in, and long forgotten gas stations. No one knows how to drive a vehicle except the Informer who occasionally rides his faded black jeep. Where does he get the gas to fuel his faded black jeep? No one knows.

Even the former post office building, now missing the letters "s" and "t," lies in rubble. No one sends handwritten letters in blue ink or black ink to any of us in District 933, and no one calls on telephones or cellular phones with weakened batteries and weak signals for us in District 933, and no one wants to hear us talk, or see the questions that linger in our eyes in District 933. Questions like those linger like the rains and the winds that stir up the red dirt filling our mouths with its richness, and so we remain locked up waiting for letters and phone calls that never come.

The Informer never socializes with any of us. He does nothing but walk the streets looking for his next recruit to send to the Nirvana Province district. He walks the streets covering the raven eyes that burn the souls of men into nothing, raven eyes that I have never seen, raven eyes that I fear to see.

The metal works man says nothing else to me, and I welcome his silence and the crackle of the fire's flame. I wave my hand and admire my gold ring, which shines in the firelight. The gold circle caresses my body like a lover and except that my finger on my left hand, the possessor of this jewel, is Deron and the ring is me, my essence. My ring, an unending circle created by the metal works man, bonds the union I have with Deron.

———◉———

LATER THAT NIGHT DERON saw the ring on my left hand, the ring finger, and remained silent as he grabbed my hands leading me to his bed. Undressing me, his hands brushed the ring. I traced his lips with my fingers allowing the hand with the ring to linger on his lips. He took my ring finger into his mouth, and he kissed my palms and the ring again. I stroked his neck and touched his brown wooden cross on plastic black string. His chest warmed my breasts, and his legs wrapped around mine. I brushed the ring against his lips again and stroked his dreadlocks. Then, I brushed the ring down his naked back. Our lovemaking made us one like the ring. The ring bonded our union and once again, I possessed the warmth of his body, the laughter of his mouth, the breath of his lungs, the manhood of his body, and the desire of his body for my body, and the spark in his brown eyes.

I loved the way the gold ring upon my brown hand complemented the deep ebony of his skin. His skin is like the deep chocolate candy from candy boxes thrown away for their insides please no one with pink, green, or red filling inside half-eaten candy. No, Deron was the deep chocolate candy that created pleasure when an eater bit inside of the deep chocolate candy, found more chocolate and found a pecan inside the tiny morsel. Loving Deron and making love to him reminded me of chocolate. He gave me shivers with just his smile. Deep chocolate candy. Deron gave me a box like that once with the chocolate so much like him, and he enjoyed watching me devour him with my mouth and eyes.

That night, Deron served me dinner on cracked plates and wine in a chipped glass. His pots had no handles, and his forks missed teeth. His towels, holes. I said nothing.

His faded denim shirt covered my body; he wore black underwear. Deron left the metallic-silver table and returned with a wide white candle and my brush. He stood behind me and brushed my shoulder-length kinky black hair. I closed my eyes and welcomed his lips again. Then he kissed the ring.

<hr />

LIFE CHANGED FOR US in District 933. Now fine clothes filled Deron's closet. At least four pairs of shiny, black boots lined his closet floor. The average man in our district was lucky to own one pair of patched boots.

When he showered, I often opened his closet and smelled his clothes. His scent of fresh soap intoxicated me. He gave me an oversized black jacket for my birthday. I never asked him how he acquired his shiny black boots, his fine long coats, or my oversized black jacket. He once told me these items were gifts from an Enforcer wanting a favor soon.

I WALKED DOWN MAIN Street on my way to Deron's one day, and a woman with a fresh cut above her eye grabbed my arm as I passed the soup line. Staying with Deron, I never worried about food as much as other people in the district.

"Why do you stay with him? Can't you see what he is? He uses people and tosses them to the side."

I removed her hand from my arm. "I don't know what you're talking about."

"Sure you do. He doesn't really love you."

I pushed her, and the look of shock that came over the woman's face surprised her as much as it surprised me.

I broke through the soup line and ran to Deron's home. I flung the door open and slammed it behind me. He sat up on the couch as I paced back and forth in front of him.

"Deron, a woman in the soup line said you use people. They all say you use people, and that's why you have all of this stuff." I waved my hands in the air as I surveyed his latest acquisitions — a radio, gold necklace, and another wooden cross on black plastic string. "And ... she said you didn't love me."

Deron looked at me and took my hand in his. His fingers stroked the ring.

"Cynthia, have I ever hurt you?"

"No, you haven't."

"I do the best I can to take care of us. We live better than the others."

He flashed me a smile revealing his straight white teeth. I said nothing but fell asleep with my head against his chest and his arm around me.

———◉———

DERON TRADED CLOTHES, food, and shoes. Sometimes I accompanied him on his business deals. We met women and men in alleys, near The Wall, or in someone's home. If a man needed shoes and was willing to trade a few cans of beans and dollar bills for the exchange, Deron found the shoes the man needed. I never saw Deron when he acquired the merchandise for his business deals, but sometimes I saw people walk around the district with no shoes, and I wondered if they had met Deron and his associates.

———◉———

I STOPPED BY DERON'S house, and let myself inside in his apartment. I opened his pantry and found crackers, cheese and wine, which I ate. The shadows deepened in his apartment and outside, but I waited for him to come home. Leaning on the couch and closing my eyes, I fell asleep. A burning sensation interrupted my sleep. I struggled to open my eyes, but the wine, which I drank earlier, tricked my body, but I mastered my body and the wine and opened my eyes to find Deron staring down at me. I sat up and smiled.

"Deron, you're home. I waited..."

"Cynthia, it's ending," he said cutting me off.

"What?"

"Cynthia, my contact, my lead to the outside, has died. He was murdered." He paced the apartment and muttered unintelligible words under his breath, and shook his head moving the dreadlocks that framed his face.

I threw the sheet from my body and walked to Deron who muttered under his breath. "Deron, what's wrong?" I reached my hand to touch his shoulder, but I pulled my hand back and stared at his back instead.

"Cynthia, it means our nice food, wine, and the clothes source has dried up. When it runs out and it will soon, we'll be joining the soup line on Main Street unless I find a new contact outside The Wall."

He hung his head, and I bit my lip. I wasn't hungry anymore.

***

DERON LOVED ME. WHEN he harbored no anger for the world or humanity, he often took my hands as we ran through the streets laughing like two teenagers. It didn't matter that we ate stale bread or some unknown meat that was probably a rodent or small cat or that the Enforcers prohibited us from leaving District 933. What mattered was that we spent our time together. Deron chased me, caught me, and showered me with kisses. The residents in the soup line on Main Street saw us and shook their heads in disgust. We ignored them and played with Deron's latest acquisition — a football.

"Catch the ball, Cynthia."

I reached for the ball and crashed into the soup line jostling people.

"Stupid bitch. Watch where you're going with that ball."

"Yeah. Watch it. You stepped on my foot."

"I'm sorry. I'm sorry," I replied, but they ignored my apologies and shoved me.

Deron witnessed the commotion and ran to my defense. The people in the soup line turned their eyes away from him as he took hold of my hand.

"You touch her again, I'll kill you. You got that?"

"You're just a street thug pawning on other people's misery. You leech," an old man said as he spit on Deron's shiny black boots.

Deron pulled a gun from his clothes and pointed it at the man's head. "Look, old man. Is there a problem?" Deron glared at the others in the soup line who lowered their eyes. "Do any of you have a problem?"

My heart pounded in my ears, and my eyes widened. I knew Deron owned a gun, but I had never seen it until now. Deron no longer held my hand, which trembled. I wiped my moist palms on my pants. I stared at Deron, but he only had eyes for the soup line crowd.

"Don't you touch her again. The lady's with me," Deron said. "Now wipe your spit off my boots, old man."

The old man kneeled and wiped the spit from Deron's boot with his sleeve. The old man stared at me, but I looked away.

"Come on, Cynthia."

I took Deron's hand again, his laughter returned, and so did mine.

———◉———

I KNEW I WAS PREGNANT with Deron's child. I hadn't had my period for quite some time, and queasiness rocked my stomach every morning. I hid my condition from him by staying in shallow light and making love in complete darkness. I stopped spending the nights with him to hide my morning sickness, but somehow he found out the truth.

"How far along are you?" he asked.

"What?" I dropped my knife onto the broken plate that had fresh bread, ham and green beans, a feast for a change. Deron had met a new contact. I brushed my fingers against my ears, and I twisted my ring.

"Don't lie to me, Cynthia."

Deron's voice frightened me. "Maybe three months," I said looking at him. I smiled. I wasn't ashamed of having our child.

His hands gripped the table for a moment then he ran his hands through his dreadlocks. "When were you going to tell me?"

"I-I don't know."

He stood up then and left the room. I sat there in front of my broken plate. My eyes watered, but I refused to cry. My hands shook, and I placed them in my lap. I left the kitchen table and went to his room to pack my things, but Deron returned ten minutes later and grabbed my arm.

"I sleep with you every night, woman. You think you can fool me? I know you, Cynthia," he said. "I know you've tried hiding your condition from me by changing in the dark and away from my eyes, but I know every curve, every hair, every scar, and every blemish. My hands know your body in the dark, my hands know your body in the water, and my hands know your body in the light. I know you and I have watched the changes in your body with interest — the swelling of your breasts, the swelling of your hips, and the swelling of your stomach. You cannot hide from me." His grip tightened on my arm, and he forced me to look at him. "But know this, Cynthia. I don't want it, and it's not going to happen," he paused. "I know someone who will take care of it."

His words echoed in my head. Had the wine dulled my hearing? Take care of it? What did he mean by that? He released my arm and paced the room like a caged animal. "I want my child," I said.

"I will not walk around this place and see an insignificant crumb snatcher with my eyes. Do you hear me?" He slammed his fist on the table, and a cracked glass fell to the floor and shattered. "This is no place for a child, Cynthia." Deron grabbed his black leather jacket and left the apartment.

After he left, I resumed my frantic packing, and I ran down the darkened street staying close to the alleys. I ignored the moans of men and women rocking cars with fogged windows to-and-fro with their passion, and I ignored the drunks who lay passed out among trash heaps. I saw my apartment but changed my mind. He would search for me there first. I turned another alley and saw the back door of the old movie theater where people who had no home often stayed. I smiled and entered the door. I passed by a man and woman kissing and hid in the balcony.

I lay on the floor in the old film room with its huge projector, film reels, and faded movie posters of an actor called Will Smith in *I Am Legend*, *Terminator 2: Judgment Day* with a man-machine named Schwarzenegger, but the last movie poster that caught my eye was *The Fountain* with a beautiful man and woman. Love never dies. These people who created these images, these films, imagined a future so different from my own. I slept with my hand with the ring pressed firmly against our baby and dreamed of the man and woman who loved each other throughout time.

DERON FOUND ME THREE days later. I woke up and found him standing over me. Two men stood behind him. They grabbed my arms while Deron took a syringe and injected it into my arm. "Why, Deron?" I mumbled before seeing darkness and Deron fade before my eyes.

I WOKE UP IN A DIMLY lit room. A white gown covered me. I touched my stomach and knew the child was gone. I reached up to my hair and found that my shoulder-length black tresses were also gone. A closely cropped spiked haircut like grass cut with a lawnmower's rusted blade met my fingers. I looked for the ring and found it intact on my hand like a hungry dog with bared teeth clutching a bone and like that dog's bone, the ring clutched my finger daring to grip my finger tighter. I tried to remove it from my hand, but it clutched my finger. I refused to look down at it on my finger. The ring's fake gold mocked me now and the metalworks man's warning echoed in my mind.

It's not true gold. It will turn, Cynthia.

AFTER MY RECOVERY FROM this violation of my body, I waited for Deron in another white room. Repeatedly, I told the woman who watched me that Deron would come for me.

It's not true gold. It will turn, Cynthia.

"He dropped me off. He's coming to pick me up," I said from the bed.

"Honey, you need to rest after ... the procedure. It's not time to leave yet," she said.

"Deron's coming. When he comes, bring him to this room," I said. "He loves me, you know."

The woman glanced at another man who looked at me with raised brows. I ignored their glances and waited, but Deron never came.

━━━━◈━━━━

MY RELATIONSHIP ENDED with Deron that day in the white room, but I wanted to see him again, so I began following Deron by hiding in the shadows and covering my face and eyes with dark shades and floppy hats. Sometimes I stood in the soup line and watched him walk past laughing with his associates. Twisting the ring on my finger, I left the soup line and trailed Deron. I stood in the alley, kissed the ring, and brushed it across my cheek allowing my eyes to feast upon him.

I watched him in the alley for several hours and watched the light fade from the sky. After he left, I leaned against the alley wall where he had stood moments before, closed my eyes, and breathed in his scent that lingered in the air. I brushed the ring across my lips, whispered his name, and pretended that the ring was Deron's mouth on mine. When I opened my eyes, a man stood in front of me.

"You look lonely, love. A pretty girl like you needs someone to care for her. You want to come home with me tonight?"

Glancing around and seeing no one else in the alley, I pulled the man's head close to mine and pressed my lips against his lips. I forced my tongue into the man's mouth and kissed him. The man responded and pressed me against the building.

"You can't wait for my room?" he said breathing heavily as his hands squeezed my breasts.

I silenced his talking with another kiss, harder this time. I reached up to stroke his cheek and accidentally scratched him with my ring.

"What the hell?" the man said touching his cheek. He backed away from me, and then ran. His steps echoed in the alley.

Banging my head against the wall, I opened my eyes and looked at the ring. "Damn you, Deron. I can't even have a man satisfy me without you tormenting me."

I walked home in the rain.

━━━━◈━━━━

THE DAY THE INFORMER chose Deron for his mission broke my heart. I saw the black trench coat wearing Informer standing across the street staring at the soup line. Dark shades covered his face, and a black wool fedora hat covered his head. A few people ahead of me stood Deron who also had noticed the Informer. Deron looked at the Informer and walked away from the soup line. I glanced at Deron then at the Informer, my breath quickened, and my hunger faded from my belly. I stepped away from the soup line and watched Deron's back as the distance widened between us. The closer he walked to the Informer, the farther away from me he became. I moved another step and tried to stop my trembling hands. I almost called Deron's name. I wanted him to reject the Informer's recruitment of him.

The old men and the old women turned their heads in disgust and spit on the ground when Deron passed. I heard their murmuring.

"The Informer chose a dishonorable man for the mission?" a woman asked.

"He's a thief, a murderer," a man said.

"The Informer's lost his mind choosing that hot head," another man said.

I wanted to speak in Deron's defense, but I pulled my hat down over my face. I wiped the tears that entered my eyes. I was so thankful that it rained. No one could see my tears that flowed even more the farther away the Informer and Deron walked. They talked and then the Informer walked away from Deron. Deron stood in the rain watching the Informer, then he walked away down the street until his black coat and long black dreadlocks became a tiny dot in my eye. Something about that moment frightened me.

Admiring him for his nice shoes and coats, young boys trailed Deron from a distance telling each other they would follow his example. When they became men chosen by the Informer, they would honor Deron's coolness. I heard their declarations and wondered if a ring, a tiny circle wrapped around a finger, and a child would choke their breath and chill their blood.

Yeah, the Informer chose Deron well. The way he held his head with those swinging black dreadlocks, smooth ebony skin and perfect teeth — he defied them. He used everyone he ever touched. The bastard.

SIX MONTHS LATER, I knew the day Deron died. The day the warmth left his body, the day the laughter left his mouth, the day the breath left his lungs, the day the manhood left his body, the day the desire for women left his loins, and the day the spark left his eyes was the day my lover died.

The day Deron died the ring slipped from my finger into my morning bath water. The gold was green, and the ring was cracked. I slipped it back on my finger, got out of the metal tub, and placed my naked, wet feet onto the cool cement floor. Water and soapsuds dripped from my body creating a puddle as I traced one crack with my fingernail.

I shivered and walked into the bedroom that I shared with three other women who worked the mines during the day. Walking past a mirror, I caught a glimpse of my reflection. My mahogany skin glistened from the water and soapsuds. My hands lingered on my stomach for a moment, and then I wiped a tear off my already slick cheek. I released the pins holding my chin-length, thick black wavy hair in place, and climbing into my twin bed, I covered my naked body with a sheet and blanket. I swallowed and hugged my pillow tight.

Later that evening, the Informer stopped by and told my roommates that Deron had died. I heard the Informer's baritone voice drift through the walls. I heard my roommates' whispers as they deliberated among themselves about whether telling me was the right thing. The Informer insisted and entered my bedroom. I kept my back to him.

"Deron's dead. I found his body early this morning. The Enforcers dumped his body over The Wall," he paused. "He made it to Nirvana Province. He brought food and medicines before they killed him."

"How did he die?" I asked from my tent of sheets.

"Will knowing change anything?"

"Tell me, Informer. How did he die?"

"He was kicked and beaten to death," he paused again. "There will be a funeral. Everyone is invited."

"His face?"

"Okay."

The Informer left my bedroom, and I clutched my pillow tighter. The Informer's visit didn't surprise me. After all, he seemed to have eyes all over town. Perhaps the old security cameras worked. He knew everything and everyone. Had Deron told the Informer about me? The Informer found his latest recruit in my lover Deron. I knew Deron had escaped our district; the Informer trained him well to infiltrate the Nirvana Province district, and I knew Deron died the day the ring slipped from my finger.

I glanced back at the ring on my finger. Had the ring choked Deron — choked his laughter, his breath, his manhood, his desire, his spark? Was the ring to blame?

Tonight, my roommates gave me the bedroom for total privacy. They rolled their bedding and slept on the floor in our living room area. I turned on my back and watched darkness fill the bedroom.

———◉———

AFTER A RESTLESS NIGHT filled with thoughts of Deron, I prepared for Deron's funeral the next morning. I bit my lip as I stared into my puffy eyes in the mirror. I threw cold water on my face again. The corners of my mouth lifted. I saw the young woman who loved Deron smiling back at me.

I dressed for his funeral touching the tarnished green ring again.

———◉———

MANY RESIDENTS MAINTAINED their manners and offered their respects at the Sunday funeral. No one worked the mines, so men came with their women and children. Curiosity brought many to hear the Informer's words. The young men, with stern eyes and naked muscled arms to show their courage and strength, dressed in their military gear hoping the Informer chose them. Others came glad to see Deron the street thug buried in the ground. Others wiped a tear when they heard the Informer's words of Deron's sacrifice for the children. The Informer led the service, which he held outside under an open sky. The day Deron died no sun shined. No sun shined now on the cloudy and warm morning.

Why did I come to Deron's funeral? Did I come to heal myself? Was it having my revenge sated? Morbid curiosity? I loved Deron and that was my mistake, I suppose. He never wanted our child and made me pay for it with my shoulder-length tresses. My hair has grown to chin-length since then, but I keep it pulled back from my face in a tiny bun.

After the white room, I often awakened to a child's crying, but I knew no child lived in the room that I shared with three other adults. Many mornings I found my pillow and hair wet, and I stared at the ring that once brushed across Deron's body. With Deron's death, I thought of our child's lost life.

As I walked by Deron's coffin, a wooden box that was his final resting place, the Informer nodded, and I stroked Deron's black dreadlocks and touched his cold lips. In death, Deron looked so much younger. Cynicism and hatefulness no longer lined his face.

I loved Deron, lost my child, and lost my mind.

Yet, I lived still and the broken ring, now green, refused to mend when I pressed the ends together. The crack remained in the ring, now green.

The Informer understood me and knew about my relationship to Deron. No, I refuse to call our encounter a relationship. We connected and created oneness, unbroken, unending like the ring. I was the only one the Informer allowed to touch Deron that morning in his wooden box, his final resting place. When the Informer asked the mourners if anyone had remarks, he glanced at me.

Giving remarks appropriate? Say nothing? What words remained in my heart that I could release from my mouth? I don't know. Other women Deron knew came to the funeral. Did they bear the same scars I did? I don't know, but I loved Deron.

I glanced at his face again, and the tears rolled down my cheeks. I touched the brown cross around his neck, his jewelry in life and now in death. The Informer dressed Deron well for his final day. Wearing his favorite black coat, and his shiny black boots, which are spotless, Deron seems asleep.

I stroked his dreadlocks and traced his lips with my fingers. Would our son have resembled him and had his defiant spirit? Perhaps our son would have changed things and made things better for everyone here. Perhaps our daughter would have made the change happen. I don't know. I touched his face once more. I removed the tarnished ring, now green, from my finger and placed it on his chest.

Yeah, I knew the day Deron died. I knew the day Deron died when I wanted to seal our bond with the ring created in fire. The day the warmth left his body, the day the laughter left his mouth, the day the breath left his lungs, the day the manhood left his body, the day the desire for women left his body, the day the spark left his eyes, was the day I knew Deron no longer lived.

I knew the day Deron died when I removed the broken ring, now green, from my finger and lived.

The Life Giver

Those boys drove their momma crazy.

It was a disgrace that Clara Donovan, a sixty-year-old woman, should walk the dark streets of Dallas clutching her black old ladies' purse that looked like a doctor's bag from one of those Western television shows. Big, black, heavy, mysterious.

Whenever someone walked the streets in the early morning hours, it always meant trouble; either somebody slipping money, passing drugs, seeking sex, or stealing things not nailed down or nailed shut. Strange things walked the streets after dark that time of the morning that was so dark the dark seemed black, looked beyond black, beyond the color of melted tar placed on streets on a hot summer's day. Dogs barked in the darkness that hid them. Only their barking and the clicking of their nails on the sidewalk or street confirmed their presence. Sometimes men slept in the darkness on the porches of the small, white wooden church near the freeway, Interstate 20, hoping to keep their demons away.

Strange things walked the streets after dark so much that people wondered if the strange things existed only at night like some vampire character from a bad horror movie.

Strange things walked the streets after dark like a woman in a blue minivan, a vehicle used for shuttling children from football and track practices to piano lessons and youth choir practice. Instead, the woman who drove the minivan parked her family vehicle at the truck stop, stepped out, locked it up, and walked up and down the sidewalk in front of the truck stop hoping the curve in her derriere and the jiggle in her top convinced the men of her desire for conversation. Besides, the mortgage was due in two weeks and she had to hurry.

Strange things walked the streets after dark.

However, the strangest thing of all that walked the streets after dark was the woman with the black handbag, Clara. Even hard heads, lost young men intent on seeking a victim, shied away from the woman who walked the streets carrying a black bag. Young brothers called her crazy and heard rumors that she killed the last hard head who tried to take her purse one night long ago when she walked the streets. No one confirmed or denied the story because everyone believed in the possibility. A woman searching for her son on Dallas' streets in the early morning hours was crazy, looking for a fight, or had beaten the devil at one in an alley. No one wanted to take a chance. Therefore, young toughs crossed the street when she passed.

Strange things walked the streets after dark.

Many times Clara interrupted their poker games, dice games, and drug deals with the same questions.

"Have you seen my son? Well, tell him I'm looking for him."

Although Mrs. Clara had three sons, everyone knew which son she searched for – Randy. She never said his name, but they knew he was the only son she searched for braving the evils of the night.

Forty years ago, her life and spirit filled with song. Once upon a time her now swollen feet, crusty from neglect, ashy from walking Dallas streets in Oak Cliff, cracked from standing long hours folding sheets and cleaning hotel bathrooms in North Dallas, filled black pumps showing off her shapely calves promising and teasing men whose eyes followed the long, black line where her dresses hit right at her calf of something more. Once her slender feet, and they had been slender, made everyone smile when she kicked off her shoes and ran barefoot like the country girl she once was a long time ago. Then, the man saw her smile, and love danced in her heart.

Before her husband began his cross-country trips, he drove his eighteen-wheeler truck on a dedicated run. The old women, matriarchs in their time, smiled and nodded their approval. Her husband, *her* man, raced home to be with *his* wife, and they called her blessed for never collecting gray hairs behind a husband who either spent the money at a bar before coming home, purchased another expensive yard appliance they didn't need, or worse gave it to another woman he kept hidden away from knowing eyes. No, Clara didn't have those troubles, so matriarchs gave her their blessings and prayers of protection. They saw hope and promise in the young couples' steps.

When her husband came home, Clara had dinner waiting for him; she massaged his temples and let him lead her in the dance. He listened with wonder when she told him what the Oak Cliff New Hope Missionary Baptist Church women's auxiliary did for the community, and she was president.

And Clara let her husband lead her in the dance.

Life was good.

Life was good until the boys came. Something changed, snapped like thread, and Clara forgot her husband's tune and their dance. Her husband had loved her much, but she had loved her sons more like a mother grizzly threatening to destroy, maim, or devour anyone or anything that harbored ill will towards her cubs, her sons. She even growled at him when he tried to discipline his children who were beginning to smell foul. The baby, Randy, was too young to exhibit such ugliness yet, like the other sons, who smelling the new strength in their bodies and reveling in their new power, tried to challenge their father like young elephant bulls wanting their share of the female herd. Like that master elephant bull, he slammed them down into submission or tried to, but she interfered in his man-father business by growling at him. He looked at the baby, grinned, and offered his prayers. He prayed for the others, but he feared for his wife and asked God for mercy. He only shook his head and continued his cross-country truck runs hoping she had enough love for him.

And love she had for him. She grieved for him when he died after their marriage of thirty years, her world unraveled, and hearing her mind come unhinged, the oak tree in her front yard wept with her. The tree that withstood tornado–like winds, severe thunderstorms, and threats of flood cracked in half, its middle split. It began to die.

Now an older woman looking for her son, Clara's love danced in her heart now on dull hardwood floors in forgotten dance studios with broken glass windows and lights that no longer lit the room. She carried that love around now in her black bag, her prison, and for anyone who showed a genuine interest, she told them about her son whose picture she proudly removed from her bra to show anyone. And like always, no one denied Clara her joy. Who could take that smile from her face when her song, a song of a young woman in love, died a long time ago? One day her love would kill them. Therefore, neighbors indulged her, talked to her, laughed with her, and remembered to tell her son to call.

NEIGHBORS LOST THEIR minds that summer.

It all started in June when a neighbors' child, Stephanie, rode her pink bike in the middle of the street yelling, and everyone rushed out to witness the police handcuff a man.

"He touched my brother! The police got the nasty man! The police got the nasty man!" she yelled.

Everyone saw the nasty man walk away holding his head down as the policemen escorted him to their vehicle.

"I told you there was something wrong with that man being all single. Didn't see too many women visiting him," Ora Lee said as she puffed on her cigarette and scratched her latest long, curly auburn wig that reached her shoulders. She looked like Donna Summer at the height of her disco days. "You girls watch out for guys like that. Single indeed."

Stephanie's family moved away before the summer ended.

Neighbors lost their minds that summer.

Two women who lived at the end of the street fought each other in the middle of the street in late June on a day the temperature tipped at 103 degrees. Everyone swore up and down that Mother Nature got confused and placed an August temperature in June when brides had their last outdoor weddings except heaven help the poor child who sat outside on this day melting under the June sun dressed in her beautiful, white wedding gown.

Someone revealed that the women were seeing the same *married* man. The women took their anger, their shame, their embarrassment, their indignation at this act of unfaithfulness in their minds and fought like men with their balled fists and punches that battered muscles, bruised skin, and discolored faces with a shade of red that would have motivated make-up artists representing the expensive cosmetic companies to run into the lab hoping to reproduce that shade of red – Scorned Red, Passion Red, Dangerous Red, Texas Hot Red – as a blush and a lipstick.

Unfortunately, the police took them away as well, and no one ever discovered the married man's identity. If he had any sense, he wouldn't stray again and if he did, he'd choose more wisely and not share his affection with two women who happened to be neighbors.

Neighbors lost their minds that summer.

After a night of walking, Clara sat on the trunk of the burgundy 1976 Lincoln Town Car eating a bowl of sweetened, multi-colored children's cereal.

Those who remembered the Lincoln Town Car being driven recalled how long it took Mr. Donovan to turn the corner. It stretched for days that when it finally made it to the corner, it was already the next day, the kids joked. The young men walking the streets saw her eating her meal at three a.m. sitting on the trunk of that Lincoln Town Car that no longer worked, her husband's old car, and they left the sidewalk and walked in the middle of the street.

She watched them, swallowed another spoonful of cereal, and asked them the question they expected every time she appeared.

"Have you seen my son?"

Only one, the tallest boy, responded. "No, we haven't seen him, but we'll tell him you're looking for him, Mrs. Clara."

She sighed, watched the young teens walk away, and returned to her bowl of cereal. She finished the cereal and watched the stars fade to morning.

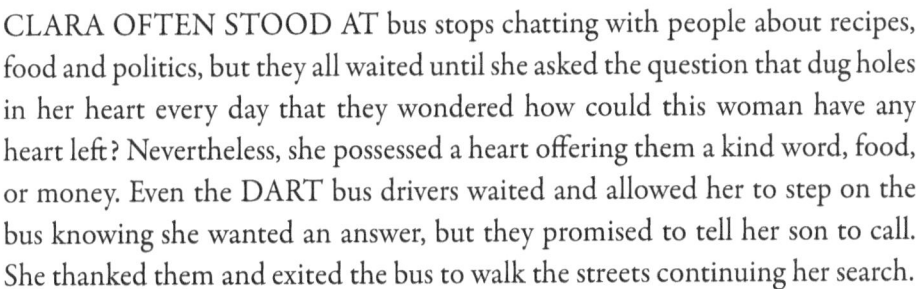

CLARA OFTEN STOOD AT bus stops chatting with people about recipes, food and politics, but they all waited until she asked the question that dug holes in her heart every day that they wondered how could this woman have any heart left? Nevertheless, she possessed a heart offering them a kind word, food, or money. Even the DART bus drivers waited and allowed her to step on the bus knowing she wanted an answer, but they promised to tell her son to call. She thanked them and exited the bus to walk the streets continuing her search.

Neighbors lost their minds that summer.

Toolboxes sitting on garage shelves disappeared. Lawnmowers filled with gas for cutting St. Augustine grass, Bermuda grass, and weeds vanished from backyards and opened garage doors. Bikes disappeared and anything left outdoors not nailed down or too heavy to pack away vanished. Neighbors whispered and watched Mrs. Clara's son Junior, the one who returned from prison in late June. No one really remembered why he went to prison in the first place, and the older neighbors who remembered the reason never told young or new neighbors. Instead, they gave warnings like lone sentinels guarding gates of long forgotten fortresses lined with mines.

"Watch out for him. Trouble is coming."

"Be careful."

"Don't let him inside your house."

"He's been to prison. He's changed."

"Why did she let him return home?"

Their talk tired Ora Lee as well as Mrs. Clara walking the streets with her black bag. Ora Lee, the countrywoman from the Deep South who no one really remembered whether she hailed from Alabama or Mississippi, maintained a constant vigil on her porch smiling at Mrs. Clara and speaking with her about mustard greens she would make for dinner that day.

Ora Lee served as the watcher, the woman who knew everything, but she never used her knowledge for mischief, only for good in her eyes. In time, everyone liked Ora Lee, who had been married twice and no longer dwelled on the business of men and romance. Romance, she scoffed, belonged to starry-eyed girls who watched too much television and read too many romance novels and older women, who should have known better, but threw caution to the wind and believed in a man's love declarations even when the signs told them he presented problems namely being married, drug addicted, unemployed by choice, or a participant in illegal matters.

As she told one woman, she had had enough of that love business and for the time being was spending her time being a good mother, making sure her children saw their fathers, serving as a band booster mom for one child who served in the high school band, serving in the church, and buying the latest wigs.

Ora Lee often sat on her porch after a long workday observing what happened on the block. She always made time for Mrs. Clara.

"Summer going to be hot this year, Ora."

"Yes, ma'am, Mrs. Clara. It's going to be a tough one this year. They're talking about a heat wave," she said taking a draw of her cigarette before putting it out. "You should come to church with me Sunday, Mrs. Clara. We're having a revival. We've got some out-of-town choirs coming. Should be wonderful."

"Church? Yeah, revivals always were nice. Something about those tambourines, drums, and holy ghost music," Clara said as she sat next to Ora and gazed down the street. "Ora, have you seen my son?"

"No, Mrs. Clara I haven't, but when I see him..." she trailed.

"Well, tell him I'm looking for him," Clara said as she stood up and stretched. "I guess I should be going home now. I need to see about dinner."

Ora glanced at the weeds at Clara's house that grew tall in her front yard. The pink paint faded in places, and her roof needed new shingles years ago. "Mrs. Clara, I can send my son over to cut your yard this weekend. He needs something to do."

"Oh, don't worry about that. Thank you. I'll get Junior to do it. He's running around here somewhere."

"Okay, well, if you change your mind."

"Okay." She waved as she walked away from Ora to the faded pink house with damaged roof shingles on top.

———— ⚬ ————

JUNIOR VIOLATED HIS parole in less than two months because of gun possession, which he tried to explain saying he didn't know it was there.

Neighbors stood outside and watched Junior walk to the police car with his hands handcuffed behind his back. Some watched with arms folded against their chests while others shook their heads. Some neighbors, out of respect for Mrs. Clara, peeped from behind closed window blinds opened a slit.

Clara knew they expected her to create a scene with crying, begging, screaming, and falling on the ground or worse, grabbing one of the officer's hands pleading, but she never glanced in her neighbors' direction. She only had eyes for her son.

"Junior, make sure you pray, son. God is merciful. Give your life to him."

"Momma, it ain't my gun," he said. "I promise I'll do better. I'll build you a new wooden fence when I return, and I'll cut the yard all the time."

She nodded and with tears in her eyes hugged her son with his arms bound in silver handcuffs behind his back. Something about that silver tarnished his beautiful brown arms. "Don't forget to pray, Junior. Jesus will save you, and I'll see you again."

The police took him away handcuffed, and Mrs. Clara stood in front of her yard and watched her oldest son ride away to prison.

Again.

———— ⚬ ————

BOBBY, ORA LEE'S SON, and his friend Jo-Jo cut the weeds at Mrs. Clara's house and repaired the fence for Junior who never came home again. He died in a fight with another inmate at the Texas State Penitentiary in Huntsville.

———◦———

EVERY DAY CLARA WALKED up and down the street clutching her black bag on her arm like a lifeline, her IV delivering the precious life-giving nutrients she needed.

Sometimes Clara walked to the truck stop near the freeway. She remembered how life had been at the park near the recreation center with Girl Scout meetings, Boy Scout meetings, class reunions, neighborhood associations, and exercise classes for women with the gym windows covered to prevent boys and men from peeking and gawking at the women in their body suits as they walked around the gym led by their instructor. She passed the old recreation center that some children and youth once called HHU, Highland Hills University, the place for basketball players who once had dreams beyond the neighborhood. Some relived those dreams while others wanted the chance for a new life. Passing the darkened park, Clara ignored whispers she heard from cars that sat parked with the shiny hubcaps that looked like mirrors under moonlight. The streetlights revealed the gleam in their mouths when the men spoke, and the men saw Clara and refused to bother her even though the three o'clock in the morning darkness hid their sins from the world.

Everyone knew those boys drove their momma crazy, and everyone left Clara alone.

Clara ignored them and continued her walk up the hill to the truck stop whose lights pierced the night like a flashlight flicked on under a sheet by a child who read his latest comic book even after his parents told him bedtime started hours ago.

The women, who sashayed back and forth in front of the truck stop searching for company and who prayed their children slept until they returned home, turned their faces in shame away from Clara hoping she failed to recognize them and if she did, prayed that she kept their secrets safe.

Clara kept their secrets. She smiled standing on the sidewalk and asked the women questions about their children while men cruised by in their cars and sped away after having second thoughts when they saw the woman those boys drove crazy standing there talking to the women they wanted to know in the biblical sense.

"I haven't seen him, Mrs. Clara," Sonya said praying that the night hid the fact that she wore no underwear under her blue denim, sleeveless dress that had buttons running from a scooped neckline to the bottom of the dress, which hit her calves.

"Well, if you see him, tell him I'm looking for him. Goodnight."

"Goodnight, Mrs. Clara."

Mrs. Clara resumed walking in the direction of the truck stop but stopped her stride in the middle of the sidewalk. Her straight back now faced Sonya.

"Sonya?"

"Yes, ma'am?"

"Come here, darling."

Sonya glanced around and walked to where Mrs. Clara stood and tried to see what caught Mrs. Clara's focus. She gazed in the same direction seeing only eighteen-wheeler tractor trailers and cabs parked with sleeping men with sleeping women and sleeping men who desired company away from the truck stop's bright lights.

Mrs. Clara took Sonya's cool hand, pressed some bills into her hand, and closed her hand over them. She sighed and glanced at the woman young enough to be her daughter.

"Sonya, go home. You shouldn't be here tonight," she said. "You're a beautiful child, and your momma wouldn't want this for you."

"M-momma?" Sonya's lip trembled, her eyes shined like glass, and the sobs erupted from her body as her shoulders moved up and down. "It's so hard ... by myself ... he doesn't ... help ... me ... the house ... trying ... to keep."

Mrs. Clara hugged Sonya and let her cry in her arms. After a few minutes, her cries subsided into soft whimpers. When Sonya broke free from Clara's embrace, she wiped tears from her eyes.

"Go home to your babies. It'll be all right."

Sonya nodded and walked back to the blue minivan. "Mrs. Clara, what about you? Can I take you home?"

"No, child. I need to talk, walk, and pray," Mrs. Clara said. She watched Sonya drive away in her minivan and walked up the hill to the truck stop's bright lights.

Sonya returned home, checked on her three children, took a shower, and saw the folded twenty-dollar bill on her bed. Opening it and expecting to see one-dollar bills folded inside of the twenty-dollar bill, she gasped when she counted the bills of twenties and fifties that amounted to one thousand dollars in her hands. The mortgage was paid for the month.

———— ● ————

"HAVE YOU SEEN RANDY, Ora?"

"No, Mrs. Clara, but I got something else for you." She opened the front door and yelled inside for her son, Bobby.

A few minutes later, Bobby came outside the house carrying a black Lab puppy. "Mrs. Clara, this is for you. Our dog Lady had a litter, and we're giving the pups away," he said.

Clara stared at the dog, which wagged its tail and round puppy fat body as it sniffed her feet. The puppy didn't seem to mind that her crusty feet, once beautiful and adorned with polish, now craved comforts Clara no longer desired.

"A puppy." She stared at the puppy and picked it up. "Thank you, Ora." She glanced at the black puppy's face, and he licked her nose. She laughed. "I'll call you Frisky. Frisky the black Lab."

———— ● ————

MARCUS AND VERONICA sat in the yard pulling weeds, which helped their dad. Veronica kneeled on her knees with knee guards while Marcus used the hoe to chop away the stubborn weeds that threatened to remain rooted in the ground despite his hacking with the hoe.

Mrs. Clara stopped in front their house and watched them work.

Veronica glanced at her. "Hi, Mrs. Clara."

She watched them a few minutes before speaking. "You children have done a good job with this yard."

Veronica glanced at Mrs. Clara's feet, which were crusted, skin peeling from her dark brown feet, her skin so dry that her feet looked white. Her flared-leg orange flannel pants met her ankles. A white, short-sleeve shirt with LBJ on the front, a faded remnant of another time, fit her like sausage casing. Her black synthetic wig, matted in several places, sat askew upon her head. That's how it was ... too much heat ... probably cooking while wearing the wig.

"Have you seen Randy?"

"No, ma'am, we haven't."

"Okay then."

She walked away down to her house.

They worked on the yard, and the sun continued to dip. It had been a long day.

THE CLOCK BUZZED AT three a.m. in Veronica's room.

"Guess it's time to get ready," she said. She walked to the bathroom, brushed her teeth, and washed her face. Returning to her room, she grabbed a pair of black navy sweats and a sweatshirt. She covered her Afro in a baseball cap.

She heard her brother rustling in the kitchen grabbing breakfast and lunch.

"Sleepy head, you ready? Ready to make that drive to Lewisville?" he said.

"Yeah, I guess so. Besides after dropping you off I can head to the gym."

They walked outside the house at four-thirty in the morning to the car parked in the driveway. The sky's black curtain contained stars still. No dogs barked. No music played. No cats pranced down the street doing their prowl. The only thing that pranced, walked, or stalked was the woman with the black purse who startled them.

She appeared out of nowhere. Veronica had her hand on the car door and stared at Mrs. Clara. Her brother looked around making sure no one jumped out of hiding who may have used the old woman as a ruse for a robbery or a carjacking.

"Have you seen my son, Randy?"

The siblings looked at each other before returning their gaze to her. The hope for a positive answer shined in her small dark eyes brightening the gloomy night.

"No, Mrs. Clara. We haven't seen him."

The light dimmed in her eyes, and she sighed holding her head down. She raised her head up again and a faint glimmer of hope brightened her face again. "Well, if you see him, tell him I'm looking for him."

"Yes, we will. We'll tell him."

They got in the car and watched her walk away down the sidewalk until she reached her house. Veronica couldn't tell if the woman went inside the house or not. The weeds grew tall there.

They pulled away and drove in silence. The only sound that broke the night's silence was the car's engine and the blinking sound of the signal light as Veronica turned.

"It's kind of sad about Mrs. Clara," Marcus said.

"Yeah, it is," Veronica said.

"You think she'll ever find Randy?"

"I don't know. I really don't know."

Red taillights greeted them as cars, trucks, and tractor-trailers flew past them on North Interstate 35. Downtown Dallas' skyline greeted them as the night kissed the morning. They turned the radio on, and the sounds of rhythm and blues floated in the car. It was just another Saturday morning and Mrs. Clara was still searching for her son.

Strange things walked the streets after dark.

<hr />

RANDY WAS MRS. CLARA'S favorite son with his coal, black skin, and tall muscular frame. He didn't look like those skinny basketball players; he was solid enough that he could have played football if he wanted to change sports. And she loved him most because he reminded her of her husband who died leaving her alone with a shadow of himself.

Randy.

Ten years ago, everyone in the neighborhood rested their hopes on Mrs. Clara's favorite son, her youngest, the one who would make it right, who would compensate and be the child and the son the others refused to be.

Junior and Big Red spent time in and out of jail, but this son, Randy, became the inspiration for the neighborhood. The coaches raved about him;

reporters always talked to him especially those who liked student athletes. He had a job at Redbird Mall working at Foot Locker, and it wasn't uncommon for scouts and others interested in him to wait until his lunch break to take him to lunch and talk about his grades, college, and of course basketball.

Randy had no need for cheerleaders with poms poms and spirit yells. He had the best cheerleader, his mother, Mrs. Clara Donovan.

But something happened between Randy and Mrs. Clara, and no one understood how life tarnished the bond.

It started when Randy won an academic and athletic scholarship to college, and he decided to stay in Texas and watch out for his mother choosing UT Austin for basketball. His friends, coaches, and scouts said he would increase his chances if he tried for Georgetown, Duke, and North Carolina by following the footsteps of Michael Jordan and others who made their leap to the NBA, fame, and riches, but Randy shrugged his head smiling with his beautiful straight teeth that Mrs. Clara never had to repair with trips to the dentist. He was born with it inheriting his father's smile. He told critics and supporters why he wanted to attend college.

"I came to get my degree in business administration and entrepreneurship. However, if I'm blessed for an opportunity in the NBA, I'll take it," Randy said.

The reporters on sports radio, television shows and the newspaper sports pages raved about their next star calling him a good kid who focused and understood the realities of basketball. Few players made the league and for those who did, there always existed the chance that a knee injury could end a career before it began.

When Randy left for college, he visited home regularly at first. After a Christmas break during his junior year, Randy returned home and discovered Red home from one of his so-called business trips. Randy never came home again after that visit, and Clara knew that day she would no longer see her favorite son. When her heart split down the middle, she tried to mend her heart with her strong will. She had loved her husband and her children the best way she knew how and now this one, her favorite, left her. Christmas never meant the same to her.

After Clara removed the Christmas tree decorations, she stopped bragging to everyone that Randy played on television. Instead, Clara became silent. Her silence deepened even more when the police found Red dead in a park in what police said had all the signs of a drug deal dispute. Junior remained in prison at the time, so he missed the funeral. She searched for Randy and did not see him at the funeral either.

Shortly after her silence, Clara started walking during the day. Everyone viewed her walk with gladness because she was finally moving on with her life now that she accepted the heartbreak instead of letting it destroy her. Clara transformed herself becoming the mother that young girls never had, and the mother young boys often wanted instead of having mothers who turned tricks with men just to keep the electric company from disconnecting the lights.

One young boy Tony resented his mother especially when he discovered that there was something really wrong when different men came to his mother's house several times a week, and he noticed the abundance of furniture, food, and even toys for him. At first, he thought it was the kindness of these men, but as he grew older, he began to understand why they refused to look him in the eye, and that's when his mother became missing several evenings a week because she worked late, she said. Instead, Tony's anger burned inside of him like a blowtorch, and he made a promise to reject women like his mother who left him frozen dinners to eat and a television with videos to keep him company.

It was Mrs. Clara's kindness, her interest in him and his schooling that kept him focused. He appreciated that she never asked about his mother's whereabouts. Because of Mrs. Clara's encouragement, he focused on his schoolwork and decided to attend college. His future wife and children would need the best.

So, he enjoyed eating dinner with Mrs. Clara on Sundays with other children in the neighborhood who often came by to eat her Sunday best that included corn bread, black-eyed peas, green beans, yellow potato salad, ribs, ham, iced tea and a peach cobbler. Sometimes Mrs. Ora Lee and other neighbors brought extra meat at the grocery store or gave her money for her Sunday meals that they attended from time to time. Everyone was polite and no one asked about Randy. If she wanted to talk about her children, they listened to her and encouraged her, but Mrs. Clara never said a word. Instead, she asked about her charges who always helped her by putting the dishes away, cutting the yard, and doing odd jobs around the house for her keeping the pink house with the crepe myrtle bushes and pansies flower bed filled with spring – blue, pink, yellow, colors of love.

Love shined in that house like a second sun.

Love shined in that house.

Love shined in.

Love shined.

Love.

Then one day, it stopped shining almost as if God moved the sun's rays to another spot. The trouble began with the visit from Tony's mother.

"I don't want Tony coming over here anymore," said his mother who came home early one evening. She stood in Mrs. Clara's living room with her hands on her hips and nails spitting from her mouth. "Tony, you are not allowed here anymore. I told you this woman is crazy walking down the streets looking for her son."

"What do you know? You ain't ever there. You don't act like a mom," he yelled as he slung his red backpack over his shoulder. "At least Mrs. Clara cares about her son."

"Tony, son, it will be okay," Mrs. Clara said. "Don't disrespect your mother. She is your mother," she patted him on his back and to her surprise, the big basketball player, who towered over her, returned her affection with a huge hug. She was sad he no longer came to visit, but he came only to say goodbye.

"Mrs. Clara, thank you for helping me. I'm going to college because of you," he said through muffled tears.

Mrs. Clara allowed him a moment to compose himself before releasing him. "Tony, you will be all right, son. Just don't forget to pray like I told you," she paused and followed his mother outside on the porch. "You will do well in school; I know you will just like..." she said leaving her statement hanging on the wind. "You will do well."

Tony's mother jerked him by his arm, and they left with Tony putting on his headphones tuning his mother out.

Later that fall, Mrs. Clara received letters and photos from him at Howard University. She stroked the photos and sent him twenty dollars in a reply letter. Maybe God was blessing her with other sons and daughters. She smiled and decided to buy stationery, plenty of stamps, and postal money orders.

AFTER THESE EVENTS, Mrs. Clara searched for her son like a quest for the Holy Grail, immortality, or gold. Her treasure remained Randy whom no one had seen in ten years. After a time, Mrs. Clara became disheveled; the children no longer came to the house for Sunday dinners.

Love's remnants lived in that house for a time until the sun stopped shining. The pansies resisted being hardy plants in Texas weather, and they could no longer survive under the anger, the confusion, the voices, the sadness, the crying, the praying, and the cursing unspoken. The pansies said enough, shrank to withered pale green stalks, and joined the old, splintered oak tree that could have told them love's grief kills.

Mrs. Clara's house also faded from the anger and hurt. It no longer was the darling of the block, but now an eyesore that people out of respect for Mrs. Clara ignored never saying anything. Instead, they offered to send their sons over to do her yard work to give them something to do.

In addition, they wanted their sons to help Mrs. Clara. The mothers became afraid because they didn't want their love to turn to poison in their son's mouths and kill them, the life giver, in the process. Instead, they reasoned, it would have been better if the poison was in their sons when they were born to choke at their breasts instead of waiting until they were men-children smelling themselves who decided to cast their mothers to the winds like discarded, dirty, worn basketball shoes with frayed laces.

They prayed that the poison flowing from 1256 would never find them.

— ◉ —

MRS. CLARA LOST RANDY ten years ago, she missed the neighborhood children who disappeared, and her house shed the tears she bottled up inside of herself. Mrs. Clara became frayed on the outside matching the disheveled appearance of her home. Her clothes clashed. She no longer took care of her feet, once her pride and joy. She wore her slippers, her flat sandals that exposed the white-crusted feet to the world. She no longer cared as she walked the streets carrying her black bag asking everyone she knew and people she didn't know the same question with the same hope each time. And sometimes people wanted to lie just to give her a moment of joy and avoid seeing the hope die on her face. Again.

They gave her a wide berth to avoid answering her eternal question or if she caught them off guard, they answered her truthfully and lowered their eyes so her look of faded hope would not haunt their dreams that night.

———— ● ————

MRS. CLARA STOPPED going to church. Instead, she maintained her relationship with God outside of His church walls. She preferred the sermons of the TV evangelists who all had beautiful hair, such perfect hair that they reminded her of slick car salesmen who sold cars with an unwritten set of rules designed to defraud the customer. Besides, she and God had had a come-to-Jesus meeting a long time ago about Randy, and she still waited for Him to answer her.

The only thing Clara had left was her black bag and her photos of her grandchildren, a ten-year-old girl and a seven-year-old boy, which she carried in her purse like a snatched dream, a legacy connected to legacy via strands of DNA, the double helix, that staircase of colorful steps. Before her mind became unhinged, she often saw the grandchildren. When the tree died, the children's crazy mother, Junior's ex-girlfriend, stopped bringing the children around.

———— ● ————

ORA LEE FROWNED WHEN she woke up that Saturday morning. She dressed and wondered why none of her wigs worked. She knew women experienced bad hair days, but today was ridiculous. Bad wig days? She started the laundry, made the children's breakfast and ate with them, then decided to take a smoke outside. She sat on her front porch and saw Frisky sitting in the front yard howling. What had happened to the dog? Outside Mrs. Clara's house, she saw the parked black Lexus, a four-door sedan. It finally stopped after circling for weeks like a shark seeking prey.

"Oh, Jesus help us," she said as she grabbed her cordless phone to call police and wrote the license number down.

———— ● ————

THE RUMORS STARTED.

Everyone wondered who owned the black Lexus sedan that drove down their street so often. First, people believed it might have been some former drug associates of Mrs. Clara's son Big Red. The car always pulled in front of the house, but no one ever left the vehicle or even rolled the window down to ask for directions. Even Mrs. Clara peeped out the window trying to see past the tinted glass to the occupants of the fancy luxury car.

On this day, the car stopped, and a tall dark-skinned man got out of the car dressed in a sports coat, and neighbors blinked their eyes and watched the man knock on the door and enter.

--------◦--------

MRS. CLARA SAW THE tall man in her living room and thanked God for allowing her to see him once more. With his clean-shaven face, muscular build, and well-tailored clothes and nice shoes, she knew that he had turned out all right. However, the way he sat in the living room, she knew Randy came for a purpose and not social pleasantries. She feared offering him water because leaving the living room required going to the kitchen, which meant leaving his presence, and she feared him walking away too soon.

"Momma?"

He reached out to her and hugged her tight, and she sensed the vase inside trying to free the tears, but she closed the lid.

"Momma, all this time I've been gone I wanted to know why you chose Red and Junior over me?"

She paused. He was picking up that Christmas moment that stopped time for her, when her life ended, and their bond severed years ago.

"Randy, they needed me more."

"Momma, I needed you too."

"Son, your brothers lost their way, and I tried to help them find it."

"Momma, why couldn't you accept that they were flawed men who would never make it outside a prison cell? They were no good, Momma. I saw that. Couldn't you see that?"

Clara saw her living room open up revealing a past she had no desire to revisit because she possessed no power to change it. The past, an old wound, its scab exposed, showed the hurt so fresh she could smell it. She saw Christmas again ten years ago. It started with an argument between Red and Randy.

"*Red, you wrong man. Why you bringing that crap around here? Around Momma? Man, you crazy or what?*" Randy asked.

Their warriors' dance began with both men leaping at each other as they pushed each other. Her husband's grown sons who towered above her pushed each other in the chest and punched each other, and her eyes widened when she saw Red pull the gun and point it at her favorite son who looked so much like her husband. She prayed and asked God to intervene and prevent this tragedy from unfolding before her eyes.

"*Step off, Randy. You meddling in things that don't concern you,*" *Red said holding the gun extended in his hand.*

"*So, it's like that. You're going to shoot me because I tell you you're wrong to do this to our Momma? How do you think this makes her feel? Her two sons like this?*"

"*Randy, it will be all right. Leave now, son,*" *Clara said.*

"*Momma, open your eyes,*" *Randy said. "Your son is not a businessman working in Downtown Dallas. He does not sell real estate.*"

"*Son, you're not here now. So, you wouldn't know what's going on.*" *She looked at Red. "Put the gun away.*"

Red lowered his gun. "Return to Austin, college boy. Who do you think takes care of Momma now?" *Red said.*

Randy stared at his mother and Red a long time. Without saying a word, he walked to the door, looked at them once more, opened the door and left.

She didn't see him for ten years and now he stood in her living room again where that offense happened so long ago. The tears rolled unchecked down her cheek. Her past faded away from her living room and she spoke to her son, her favorite, her love returned.

"Son, you were asking me to write them off. I couldn't do that to your brothers."

"They used you, Momma."

"You don't understand a mother's love. It's unconditional, and it's the closest thing you'll find this side of heaven close to what is God's love for us."

"Momma, I hated them for breaking your heart every time the police came by the house or someone arrested them for being a suspect in something," Randy said. "You didn't deserve that, and I let them know it."

"It wasn't your place to let them know it. That was my place."

"What hurt Momma more than anything is that you defended them when they were wrong as two left shoes. You told me to back off and stay out of it."

"Son, you're not better than they were. You were flawed too. How could you cut off all ties with me? Who encouraged you? Sacrificed everything so that you could go to those after school summer programs making sure you received the best academic training you could get?" Clara asked. "Lord knows, I made my mistakes, but by your father's name and my God, I did my best. You have no right to judge me. I am your mother. What you do with it is your choice."

Randy stared at her then lowered his head looking at the floor. "Momma, I can't change what happened, but I can only talk about the future. I'm sorry for hurting you, and I want your forgiveness."

"Son, I love you, and I forgive you. Forgive me for hurting you too," she said muffled in her son's chest.

"I know we have a lot of rebuilding and catching up to do," he said. "I want you to move to Austin. Leave this house and move somewhere close so I can keep a watch on you."

"Son, you want me leave your daddy's house? After all the hard work he put into buying this house?"

"Momma, we don't have to sell it. We can set it up as a rent property for you. It can stay in the family. And I want to place Junior's children in private school. I want custody of the children. "

Clara looked at her son and smiled.

"Regardless of what Junior may have done, I want my niece and nephew to have a better life," Randy said. "Momma, I need you too and your other grandchildren need you too."

"Other grandchildren?" She blinked back the tears.

"Sharon and I have one daughter, Monet, and we're getting married next month, and I want you there," he paused. "She's the reason I'm here."

She stared at him and smiled, the room brightened, and the pansies ghosts smiled because they knew love could heal. She walked away leaving her youngest son standing in the living room as she went to her room to retrieve her black bag.

YEARS LATER EVERYONE remembered Mrs. Clara and those who barely knew her wondered if she died, moved away, or ever found her son. They all looked for a woman with a black bag who walked the streets after dark, but they never saw Mrs. Clara again, and they never stopped talking about her. With each retelling of her story, she became more heroic, a tragic figure, a champion for mothers who nursed wounds behind sons and daughters who dug spikes in their mothers' hearts each day. No mother wanted children to drive her crazy like Clara's boys.

Those boys drove their momma crazy.

It was a disgrace that a sixty-year-old woman should walk the dark streets clutching her black old lady's purse.

It was unthinkable that woman approached strangers and people she knew asking the same question every time with hope in her voice that made even the toughest man, pause, swallow, and glance at his latest designer sneakers before returning her penetrating gaze and answer in a faltering voice.

"I haven't seen him."

As always, she walked away as nighttime kissed the morning in farewell. Crickets chirped. Dogs barked. A car started in the distance. A woman laughed. Clara walked on blending into the night clutching her old ladies black purse, her doctor's bag.

Those boys drove their momma crazy.

Mrs. Clara never found Randy.

Randy returned home to his mother.

Ragamuffin

Queen watched the crowds gather. Horns honked when pedestrians took their time crossing the street, and pigeons followed those pedestrians with hopes that a few crumbs would fall at their feet.

It was a warm September day, but Queen didn't mind. She could sleep outside without worrying about freezing on the cold ground. Lunchtime. Queen sighed as she reclined on the city park bench. He would come soon. She could hardly wait.

A man and woman holding hands saw her sitting alone on the bench but veered off in a different direction away from her. Queen heard their whispers. She saw the disgust in the man's eyes and his upside-down smile. A group of teen-age boys walked past with their colorful athletic shoes, wide legged blue jeans, and baseball caps sporting the Dallas Mavericks and the Dallas Stars and the Dallas Cowboys logos. They talked about football and girls without glancing her way. A man wearing dark shades and a grey suit quickened his pace when he walked past her.

They all saw Queen but ignored her. They saw a thing, not a person. She brushed her hand across her green-plaid flannel shirt and checkered, orange wool pants. She looked down at her dirty tennis canvas shoes and saw her big toes peeking through tiny holes. She caressed her coarse, matted hair and pulled her black wool cap closer on her head. She wore the cleanest outfit she owned for him. Queen knew her appearance embarrassed him, but he remained silent. She knew the other people despised her for bothering a decent man during his break from a hectic job, but he never said a word about her attire. He showered her with kindness.

Earlier that morning, Queen bought a sausage biscuit and orange juice at the fast food restaurant with the two dollars a man gave her yesterday. After eating, she washed herself with the liquid green soap. She wanted to smell clean. Queen refused to let her body offend him. She hated her smell when she went days without cleaning herself, and the sharp odor of filth and old clothes annoyed her nostrils and others. It made others who walked past hold their breath or vacate an area where she or others like her had been. The smell was a stain, a trademark she tried to shake away, but each day it reared its ugly head to cover her with stench. It reminded Queen of her place, her status.

One woman gave Queen a bottle of deodorant when she washed her hands in the restaurant's bathroom last week. Queen thanked the woman for her kindness and walked away.

Was the green liquid soap enough for today's warmth? She lowered her head, lifted the collar of her shirt, and sniffed. No fancy fragrances anointed her body only the green liquid soap. At least she smelled clean, and they would talk again.

She looked down the path he normally walked and squinted. Her eyes widened and a smile crossed her face when she saw the tall man saunter her way. He carried his lunch and some for her as well.

He sat down beside her on the bench and passed her a box of chicken. "And how is Miss Queen today?"

"Well, Miss Queen is fine today. How are you, Samuel?"

"You just refuse to call me Sam, huh? Well, that's okay. Eat your lunch."

Samuel spoke to her when she was sitting on the bench one day nearly a year ago. She thought someone else was the recipient of his warm greeting, but he had insisted upon her. The friendship brought a comfort Queen hadn't known in a while, and she wanted comfort and peace at any cost. Even if the comfort was the short-lived lunch hour or the solace she found in a liquor bottle, she needed comfort. Samuel's friendship made her bear the painful memories that refused to be buried in the deep night. She woke up screaming from the nightmares. Her erratic sleeping habits angered her other brethren who called her a drunk and a crack head.

Queen stared at Samuel and realized how handsome he was. The green eyes sparkled against his brown skin. She listened to Samuel. He had gotten a promotion. He wanted to get married. He really liked a girl and feared feeling that way for her. He questioned her the way a brother questions his sister when he wants to know about the ways of women. Why did women play hard to get? Why do women ignore you when you like them? What must a man do to win her heart? Queen chuckled as she wiped the corners of her eyes.

Samuel heard her and smiled. "Miss Queen, what you think I should do?"

"I think you should love her and see what happens."

"What if she doesn't respond?"

"Oh, she will."

They watched the cars whiz past the park. An ambulance howled in the distance. What was it Samuel gave her? Hope and peace? Comfort. His presence silenced the voices that threatened to drown her. She found the voices silent and buried when she visited with him.

The homeless called her Queen B because she acted like she was better than the other homeless people. She walked with her head high and her back a little too straight. Samuel amended her name by adding a courtesy title. Many people were so unlike him. The others scorned those who were not of their world. No transportation, no wealth, and no sanity echoed the scream of the enemy in their eyes, but Samuel's eyes embraced her; he saw no faults.

"Samuel, isn't it time you be heading back to work now?" She saw many park visitors returning toward downtown. She turned her head and wiped the tear that threatened to betray her. She took a deep breath and turned around to see him standing up looking in the direction of town.

"I guess it is that time, huh?"

"Time flies. You know that Samuel."

"It flies when you're having fun. I'll see you Monday." He waved goodbye to her and returned to downtown.

Queen watched his back until it became blurry. She blinked, and he appeared clear for her again. When he turned the corner, she placed her bags on the bench and watched the cars.

<hr />

SAMUEL NEVER CAME TO the park on weekends, but Queen came to their bench anyway. She loved sitting and remembering their conversations. Laughter interrupted her thoughts. In the center of the park, a couple with two children stood near the bronze stallions. The man took pictures of them. Queen walked closer to them. Something about the family and the camera fascinated her. She watched the man's camera click constantly as the two girls and their mother altered their poses.

"We love you, Mommy. We'll never leave you," the girls said when she kissed them on their cheeks.

We'll never leave...

A spasm crossed Queen's face as she stared at the children. Blood rushed to her head making her dizzy. She sat down on the bench, closed her eyes, and unbuttoned three buttons of the flannel shirt. Sweat rolled down her bosom. She opened her eyes and saw the children playing again. She shut her eyes again hoping the children disappeared. Queen's hands trembled as she refastened the buttons on her shirt. She looked at the children once more and walked away from the park. The nightmare could not happen here, not now in broad daylight.

We'll never leave...

Tears blurred Queens B's vision, and she stumbled on a sprinkler. She landed on the grass with a thud and lay there a few minutes. She grabbed her bags and ran this time. The children's laughter reached her ears and seemed louder. She ran across the street and heard a car come to a screeching halt.

"You damn drunk! Get out of the street!"

Queen ran. She never looked back at the man who hurled insults at her.

———◉———

QUEEN GROANED AND HELD her head. She rolled over on her mattress and looked at the nearly empty bottle of liquor next to her. Her eyes widened. It would make the pain and memories disappear again. She opened the bottle to drink, but an image of Samuel popped in her mind. She closed the bottle and threw it in the corner of her cardboard lean-to. She glanced at her few belongings and noticed nothing missing. None of the others bothered her things. Good. She would fight them as she had done in the past. They left Queen alone and gave her respect. They called her a crazy woman.

She lay on her back and listened to the sounds of their city within the Dallas city limits — Shantytown. Mostly men lived here, but there were some women and children. They all had stories to tell. Shantytown welcomed them all with open arms — the drunks, the crack heads, the mentally ill, the jobless. No one stared at them with loathing. No one raided their cardboard houses. No one evicted them for failure to pay rent. No one worried about drive-by shootings. Shantytown offered a new life for many of them. She heard men cursing and two women arguing about who would sleep on the mattress today.

Another woman pushed a basket full of cans to trade for food or a sip of liquor. Shantytown was multicultural. Several people spoke different languages creating some confusion, but the barter system worked well here. A gesture here and a fair exchange made the language barriers less difficult.

Every now and then, a preacher with some of his church workers would set up a kitchen and feed the residents of Shantytown. During the meal, he preached for them to abandon the drugs and alcohol and come to Jesus. Some of the residents took the food and ran while others said amen and listened to the preacher. Sometimes Queen listened to him, but he reminded her of things she wanted to forget.

The rumble of wheels against the gravel made Queen glance at her can collection. No one took her cans; she sighed in relief. She had no desire to fight with anybody today.

Her stomach growled. Finding food on Sundays proved to be a challenge for Queen. She gathered her things, tugged her hat on her head, and stopped when she heard a man speaking. Something about his voice sounded familiar. His speech flowed unlike those with the slurred speech of drunkenness. She peered from a crack in her lean-to and closed the flap. Why was he here? Samuel visited her only during the week. She blew her breath on her hands and sniffed. Yeah, her mouth smelled like liquor. Would the people tell him she was here? She rummaged in one of her bags and found a piece of peppermint candy. She popped it in her mouth.

She opened the flap a slit and saw one man point in her direction. She closed the flap and brushed her clothes as neatly as she could.

"Miss Queen, you there? It's me, Samuel."

Queen hesitated. If she remained silent, he would go away without entering her small dwelling. Why did he come here today invading her privacy? They only met in the park for lunch. She never showed up at his home. She sat down on the mattress and folded her arms across her chest as she bit her lower lip. She looked around her small dwelling, saw the liquor bottle, and shoved it under the mattress.

When Queen emerged from her lean-to, she saw Samuel walking away. She closed the flap and walked toward him. "Samuel. Samuel. It's me, Miss Queen."

Samuel stopped walking and turned around. He smiled and Queen returned his smile. He always made her smile almost like...like. She shuddered and banished the memory. Not now. It would not poison this moment for her. The voices remained quiet as she stood in Samuel's presence. Leave me alone, Queen thought.

Queen reached Samuel, and they resumed walking. She glanced at him from the corner of her eye and frowned when she saw the lines in his forehead.

"Miss Queen, I know we only chat during the week, but I thought I'd come by and do something really special for you."

Samuel walked with his hands in his pockets. He looked straight ahead.

She touched his arm. "Samuel, what's wrong, baby? You look like you lost your best friend."

"We'll talk over dinner," Samuel said.

Samuel opened the door of his car for Queen, and they drove listening to the radio. They laughed and talked, but this meeting between them felt different. She fidgeted in her seat; her stomach twitched. Change it whispered. She wiped her mouth and closed her eyes for a moment. She needed a drink. The fiery liquor always killed the anxiety, the twitches, and the nightmares.

SAMUEL SURPRISED QUEEN with his invitation for dinner. She had never asked before, and he had never offered. Their lunches satisfied her soul. He saw past her dirty clothes, her bags, and her matted hair that he knew lay beneath the hat. He saw Queen, a human God created also.

Samuel showed her a room and bathroom. He told her to bathe and take as long as she liked. He even said she could play the bathroom radio. Dinner would be ready soon.

A black fleece warm-up suit lay on the bed. A bath? Queen couldn't believe it. How long had it been since she had a bath? She entered the bathroom and quickly shed her dirty clothes. She looked at the forest green attire of the bathroom and smiled. So, Samuel had taste. She picked up the yellow scented soap and sniffed it. No more sterile, green stuff. She filled the tub with water and ran her hands under the hot water. When she saw the bottle of bubble bath, she squealed. She poured the pink liquid in the water and watched the bubbles swirl into small clouds upon water.

Queen took the green hand towel on the toilet and slid in the tub. She sighed and closed her eyes. After soaking for a few minutes, she dipped her head in the water and washed her hair. Clean and soft. Queen felt the dirt slide from her hair and body underneath the bubbles as the jazz relaxed her.

After the bubbles faded, Queen saw the darkness of the water and frowned. For the next few hours, Queen would no longer be homeless. She released the plug and watched the dirt flow down the drain. She washed the tub and filled it again with fresh water and bubble bath. She slipped in again and sighed as the bubbles and hot water tingled her skin.

The wrinkles on her toes and fingers didn't bother her. Queen was clean.

Finally, she released the water and watched with some satisfaction that the water was not dark grey with grime. She cleaned the tub and dried her hair and body. She sat on the toilet stool and rubbed lotion on her body. It felt like silk against her skin. She sniffed the bottle again and laughed while the music played. She saw the unopened toothbrush and toothpaste and brushed her teeth. An old towel served as Queen's toothbrush. It cleaned her teeth, but not as well as a toothbrush. She swished the mouthwash in her mouth and felt her mouth tingle. The alcohol disappeared. Samuel could eat with her, and not be offended by her smell.

Queen washed her face and dried it while looking in the mirror. Her bronze skin glowed. Her hands touched her full breasts and her stomach, and she turned around to look at her shapely behind. She was a woman. Where had this woman been? Queen touched the reflection in the mirror.

Queen stopped looking in the mirror and looked at the radio. The jazz filled the room, but this particular song caught her attention. The image of the radio blurred as tears filled her eyes. The song brought memories of another life — part of the nightmares. Why did the nightmares threaten to hurt her now? But she couldn't think of that now. That life no longer existed.

When Queen emerged from her bath, she dressed. She put on the clean socks and marveled that the shoes fit her exactly. She wriggled her toes in the shoes and put her hands on her hips. No holes this time. No natural made air vents. Samuel had thought of everything. Cotton underwear and a sports bra, which was the next best thing considering he didn't know her size or did he? She touched her ample bosom and chuckled.

She picked up scissors and cut her matted hair. After she finished, she sported a closely cropped Afro. She brushed stray hairs in place.

Queen examined herself in the mirror. Slim and the others in Shantytown would no longer recognize this woman. They'd probably think she was one of those weekend missionaries preaching about redemption and the sins of drinking, smoking, and gambling. No, she was no preacher woman. She looked like somebody's momma.

We'll never leave...

Queen rubbed the goose bumps on her arms. Her skin grew clammy. The voice never stopped. It chased her in dreams, and now it haunted her daylight hours. She put on the jacket and zipped it up to her chin. Shantytown welcomed people who wanted to hide, who wanted to run, who wanted to survive. Shantytown welcomed Queen. Shantytown let people hide from their pain. Slim had said that one fall night last year while they stood around a trash barrel of fire. Demons don't walk near Shantytown. Angels didn't either. However, her demons chased her daily.

She brushed aside her dark thoughts and opened the bedroom door. The aroma of home cooked food made her mouth water and her stomach rumble.

"Samuel, what you in there cooking?" Queen sat on his couch and watched him put plates and steaming bowls of food on the table.

"Miss Queen, I'm making you a special dinner. I'm making my momma's New Year's dinner." He kept walking from the kitchen to the dining room.

"What you mean New Year's dinner, baby? It's almost October."

He stopped arranging dishes on the table and walked into the den. He extended a hand to her and escorted her to the table. He pulled the chair out for her and placed a napkin on her lap. Samuel took his seat at the opposite end of the square table.

Samuel wasn't kidding about New Year's dinner. Dishes containing black-eyed peas and cornbread, seasoned ribs, corn-on-the cob, and a peach cobbler covered the table. Queen's stomach rumbled louder.

"Miss Queen, my mother always served this on New Year's Day. She said it was a blessing to see another year. She believed the way you start your year is an indication of how it'll end up."

Queen remembered what she had done New Year's Day. One of the drifters, a new one to Shantytown, barged into her lean-to demanding sex. He claimed

Queen had given him the eye and that she wanted it as much as he did. The fool. He didn't know he was messing with Queen B. He succeeded in wrestling her down on her mattress, but he would get no closer to her for sex of any kind. A whack to his head with a longneck beer bottle and a kick to his groin ended his lofty dreams. He crawled out the door. When the others saw him slinking away and Queen standing there holding a longneck beer bottle, they laughed at him. Drifter never bothered Queen again. She didn't play.

That had been New Year's Day. She didn't want to spend the end of the year fighting off another drunken fool.

"You believe that Samuel? That we spend our year the way we begin it?"

"Course I do Miss Queen, but I believe that today is the beginning for a new start. Let's say grace."

AFTER THE MEAL, QUEEN rested her elbows on the table as she looked at the half-empty dishes. Samuel was so kind. He always had been. Why? She remembered his sadness earlier and swallowed. Was it that girl? Did she break his heart?

"Samuel, what's wrong? You've been laughing and talking with me all evening, but you're preoccupied. What's wrong? "

Samuel sighed and rubbed his hands across his short hair. "Miss Queen, I've never really pried too much about your past life. I only know you're different from others in Shantytown. I don't know what happened in your life that led you to Shantytown." He paused. "What I'm saying is I want you here and not on the streets this winter."

"Samuel, I-I don't know what to say. You don't have to do this."

"You're right, I don't have to do anything. I want to."

Queen removed her elbows from the table and fidgeted with her hands. She looked at the potholders hanging on the cabinet doorknobs. The white tile sparkled. Queen looked into the den. Newspapers and magazines covered the table like a miniature newsstand. The remote control to the large screen TV lay on the coffee table as well. Queen faced Samuel.

"Samuel, why?"

"I'm leaving, Miss Queen."

"Leaving? What do you mean?"

"My job transferred me to Kansas City effective Monday. A company apartment has been furnished for me. I was told after lunch Friday."

Queen stared at Samuel. Leaving he had said. Like a bad habit, her hands reached up to pull her hat down on her head, but she forgot she no longer wore it. Why did he have to leave? His company had been the highlight of her day. Queen reached for her tea glass and drank the cool liquid to ease her throat's dryness. Samuel watched her. What was she supposed to say or do?

"Miss Queen, you're welcome to stay here for a while. I'm going out of town in the morning, and I'll be back in two weeks."

Queen watched him stand up and stretch. "Samuel, you don't even know me. I can't stay here in your home."

"God knows you, Miss Queen. And I know you more than you think."

Queen watched his lean form disappear down the hallway.

———◦———

TWO DAYS AFTER SAMUEL'S departure, Queen left the comfort of his home. Home. Shantytown had been the only home she'd known now. She pulled her jacket tighter to her as she walked down the street. Queen missed Slim and the others. Besides, she missed Slim's life talks. More importantly, she felt guilty staying in Samuel's house in a warm, soft bed with a full stomach. She knew so many of the women had trouble feeding their children. As Queen neared Shantytown, she took a deep breath. Tonight, the children would eat well.

As she neared the familiar overpass and sparsely covered lawn, Queen swallowed. Shantytown served as her home, her refuge. She heard children playing. She heard a baby crying. She saw the men pushing their baskets of cans. She saw the women with their plastic bags. As Queen walked closer to Shantytown, two little boys ran past in their chase game; she watched them and smiled. The leader, who ran into the street, turned around to taunt his follower.

Queen stopped smiling. Her brown eyes widened in alarm as the driver of the white suburban weaved across the lanes as he neared Shantytown. She saw the child's eyes widen as he stared past his friend who stood in the street. Queen dropped the bag of food and ran in his direction. She yelled and waved her arms. "Get out of the street, baby! The truck! Get out now! Hurry!"

The boy noticed Queen too late to avoid the tinted-window suburban. Queen heard the thud and saw his small body roll in the street. The suburban rumbled by faster and disappeared onto the freeway ramp.

Queen reached the child and cradled him in her arms. "No, God. Please God. Not the baby. He's only a baby, God. Please, God not again." Her voice wavered as she rocked him and stroked his face. Queen could no longer feel his heartbeat. She could no longer feel his breath on her arm. Her stomach contracted into a tight ball and her tears fell on the child's face.

"Please, God. He's just a child. He has a life to live. Come on, baby. I brought food for you to eat today. You got to have your supper today."

Shantytown residents surrounded Queen offering comfort, but their faces blurred as her tears cleaned the child's face. Queen still rocked the boy when the police car pulled alongside her. She heard an officer mumble something in his radio while the second one tried talking to her. She ignored his questions and held the child tighter.

When the paramedics arrived dragging the stretcher, she closed her eyes. One of the paramedics released her arms. She watched them try to revive the child, but Queen knew even before they did that he died in her arms. When they zipped the black bag over his face, Queen fainted.

"Is she the mother?" One of the paramedics asked as he attended Queen.

"No," the officer replied. "Lives here."

The paramedic saw the bag of food and shook his head. "Where's his momma?"

"Strung out. That's what the other boy said. Strung out."

"Was he just standing in the street or what? Did he try to get out of the truck's way?

"His friend said he was deaf."

————— ◉ —————

QUEEN OPENED HER EYES and closed them to ward off the white glare. Her body ached. She opened her eyes again slowly until they adjusted to the brightness of the room. Some disinfectant filled the air. White walls and privacy curtains greeted her eyes.

Why was she here? She remembered walking to Shantytown with the food when she saw the boys playing then... her eyes watered. She closed her eyes banishing the boy's death. When she opened them again, a little boy in a white hospital gown starred at her. He held a blue ball in his hands.

We'll never leave...

Queen ignored the voice and managed to smile at him.

"You gonna sleep all day?" he asked.

"Sleep? No."

"They don't know I'm down here in ER. I keep sneaking away."

"Why are you in the hospital?"

"They said I needed to be." He bounced the ball a few times then walked closer to Queen. "You leaving soon?"

"I hope so, but my body aches all over." Queen said. "What's your name?"

"They call me Ronny."

"Queen B."

"Like a bee that flies on flowers?"

"Yeah." Queen smiled.

"You know, you talk in your sleep."

"Me? What makes you say that?"

"Queen B, who are Anthony and Sherry? You were calling for them earlier. Those your kids or what?"

We'll never leave you, Momma.

Queen gulped and sank deeper into the pillows. She stared past the boy whose mouth moved, but she no longer heard his words. She wiped her sweaty palms on the bed. Those names never passed her lips after the funeral. No one had mentioned those names. The little boy's death brought the nightmare to life again. She no longer saw the dead child's face anymore, only Anthony's face and Sherry's face.

We'll never leave...

And the nightmare, the reminder, reared its ugly head laughing at her. She reached for her liquor bottle but remembered that she was in the county hospital ER, not her cardboard lean-to. She knocked the water pitcher and cup to the floor. The phone ringing in the night. Would someone make it stop? She covered her ears with her hands blocking out the phone's ring. Yes, blocking it out would keep her nightmare at bay, but the phone rang louder in her ears. She wanted a drink, no, she needed a drink to bury the pain. The alcohol caressed her like an old lover. Yes, she needed a drink. Then everything would be okay again. She would forget it all.

We'll never leave... The voice mocked her.

"No, let me be," Queen wailed. "No, please go away. Slim, help me! Samuel!"

She heard the ominous ring again as clear as if their deaths had happened yesterday. Queen closed her eyes ignoring the voice and the visions that flashed in her mind. The visions grabbed her dragging her to that fateful day. Only this time she had no refuge. Her liquor bottle was gone. She saw herself and everything that spring day one year ago.

The car wreck, the fire.

Dead upon impact.

Home alone when the call came.

Her husband, daughter gone.

She covered her ears with her hands again. She wanted to forget. Remembering hurt too much.

Queen screamed.

The boy's mouth stopped moving. He walked closer and touched her arm. She screamed louder. The boy backed away and put his hands on his ears, and his blue ball fell to the floor. Queen screamed again until her stomach hurt. Tears rolled down her cheeks. Her body locked into a fetal position, and she let out a strangled cry while two nurses arrived and held her down. A third checked the boy.

Queen ignored the hands that touched her. She hardly felt the needle prick her skin. Her scream softened into a whimper. The sky blue uniforms of the nurses blurred in her vision. She heard the little boy's voice again, and it echoed as she sank into darkness.

"Anthony and Sherry. She asked for Anthony and Sherry."

QUEEN HEARD HER DOOR creak and opened her eyes to see the little boy, Ronny. He tiptoed in and closed the door behind him.

"You're not going to scream again, are you? I mean are you better?"

Queen watched him stand by the door. His hand rested on the handle. "I won't hurt you, Ronny."

He took a step forward. "Queen B, the nurse said you're sick, but it's a different kind of sick. Is it one of those lady things? My mom always said ladies get sick a lot. Is that true?"

Anthony had teased her about women and PMS. Her retort was that men had their PMS times too. Queen started to speak but was interrupted by another visitor. The man's white coat swished slightly as he came closer to the bed. He stared at the boy.

"Ronny, sneaking away from your room again?"

"Uh, no. I was just visiting. Ask Queen B."

The doctor raised an eyebrow as he looked at Queen. "So, Queen is your name," he paused. "Ronny, why don't you go back to your room? I've got to talk with Queen, okay?"

Ronny sighed and opened the door but waved to Queen before closing it.

"Ronny's in a foster home and comes for treatment. We've sort of adopted him here. I'm Dr. Livingston and you are Queen B?"

"That's what Shantytown residents call me."

"Miss B, we need to get in touch with your family to let them know you are here."

Queen lowered her eyes and stared at her hands. "I'll be okay, doctor. So, what do you need to tell me?"

"You can leave today, but I'm concerned about your mental state. Have you experienced a trauma recently? Has someone close to you died?"

Queen listened for the voice and found it silent. No one had called her momma or honey in such a long time. She shed no tears at the funeral. Queen nodded her head. "My husband and daughter were killed in a car accident a year ago."

The doctor sat down. "I'm so sorry for your loss. Have you ever sought grief counseling?"

"You wouldn't call it formal counseling, but alcohol can soothe the nerves, but only for a time."

"Before you're discharged, I'm referring you to the psychiatric ward for 24-hours, and after that AA. Dr. Sneed will take care of your needs now."

"I want to see a minister right now. Is there a chaplain? It's time to move on anyway."

<hr />

ONE WEEK LATER, QUEEN sat on the city bus, which she hadn't ridden in a long time. Samuel had been kind, if not a little foolish to leave her some money. She stepped off the bus and watched it roll away. She zipped up her jacket, pushed her shades closer on her face, and gazed down the street. Many of the houses curved driveways were empty. It was mid-morning and none of the residents would be home until later that evening. As she moseyed down the sidewalk, brown and gold leaves crunched under her feet. The leaves covered the well-manicured lawns. Queen looked at the sky and frowned. She hated dreary days. The cloudy sky dampened her mood. She wanted sunshine on her face, but the weather dictated otherwise.

Queen kept walking until she stopped in front of one house. She pulled her hat closer on her head and stared at the house. Unlike the other lawns, this house was unkempt. A sprinkler lay in the brown grass. The brown paint peeled in places. The storm drain hung so loosely that a strong wind would tear it from the house. Oil stains covered portions of the driveway. Uneven hedges covered the windows. Closed curtains and blinds blocked out the overcast sky. She walked up the curving driveway and stepped on the porch. Faded floral designs covered the welcome mat. Welcome to the Malreys was stenciled on the mailbox.

Queen's hands shook as she stood on the porch. A trickle of sweat slid down her arms. She swallowed. There was no turning back. She knocked on the oak door and heard no answer. She leaned forward and pushed the bell. Silence. Queen bit her lip and looked around to see if anyone watched. She retrieved a silver key on a chain from her pocket. She inserted the key into the lock, and the door opened.

As soon as she entered, Queen rested her back against the door and glanced around the darkened room. After her eyes adjusted, she saw furniture covered with sheets. Queen walked down the darkened hallway until she came to the first room. She opened the door and turned on the light. Good. An automatic draft paid the bills still. Did they think she would ever return? She had no intentions, but the child's death...Queen hoped the caretaker was off today. She needed no confrontation.

She knew this room. Lacy pink curtains and pink walls greeted her eyes. A pink lacy spread covered the bed. Six dolls lay on the bed. A large stuffed polar bear sat in the corner. Queen picked up one of the dolls and rubbed the hair. She held the doll a moment in her arms then replaced it on the bed. She sat down and stroked the bedspread.

She walked down the hall and entered a larger room. Jade and black lacquer furniture accented the room. She smiled. She had argued against this trendy furniture. She ran her hand against the shiny dresser's surface. Several cologne bottles were half-filled. She picked up one bottle and sniffed. The scent flooded her with memories. She saw him dancing and heard him laughing. She felt his lips on her ear. She looked at the bed. They made love so much in the bed and on the floor. She walked to the closet and touched his jacket that smelled like after-shave. She closed the closet and picked up the picture on the dresser of the three of them together.

"You never left me; I left you," Queen whispered as her hand stroked the picture frame.

SAMUEL LEANED BACK into the sofa as Queen told him her story. "Miss Queen, I-I well... whew," he faltered. "I knew you were special, but I had no idea that you suffered so much."

Samuel reached for Queen, and she allowed him to hold her. No one had held her in so long and she sighed. After a few minutes, they pulled away from each other.

"You helped me, Samuel. You showed me that beyond my pain I was still a human being. You didn't let my appearance turn you away. I have a long way to go to rebuilding my life now. There's counseling and other readjustments, but I will make it with the Lord's help." She paused. "Samuel, my real name is Juanita Malrey, but you can call me Queen still."

"I want to call you Queen."

Queen smiled this time as she remembered Anthony and Sherry. She wanted to talk about them now. Samuel listened to her laugh as she talked about her life with the man who was her childhood sweetheart. They disliked each other as children, but things changed when puberty set its course. Samuel's laughter warmed Queen's heart as she talked about her husband and daughter.

<hr />

QUEEN RETURNED TO THE county hospital to visit Ronny. She didn't even know his last name. Queen stood at the nurses' station and explained who she was and why she wanted to see the boy. The nurse looked through some charts and shook her head. A last name, the nurse needed a last name. Queen started to turn away from the desk in frustration when she heard a voice down below.

"You looking for me?"

It was Ronny. Queen smiled and kneeled to his level. "How did you know I was looking for you?"

"Oh, I'd knew you'd come back, Queen B. I just knew you would."

The two of them walked down the hall in silence and stopped in front of huge windows overlooking the city.

"Ronny, I wanted to thank you. You have helped me a lot."

"You think I helped you? Wow!" He watched the clouds in the sky. "Queen B, my mother would have liked you. She would have said you were a friend to have forever. I haven't forgotten her Queen. She watches over me in heaven."

Queen nodded. She held his hand as they watched the sun stream through the windows.

Night Moves

The wind wakes me. I turn on my right side, watch the sheer gold curtains flutter in the night air, and take in deep breaths. Night air reminds me of rain, it smells like summer, it smells like promises of tomorrow, and it resembles moonlight that touches my room like a mother covering her child for sleep.

The wind wakes me.

I stand by the window and it's quiet. The curtains flutter in the night air so early in the evening. I hear a car cranking and a dog barking. I hear the swish of jump rope hitting the carpet and a few minutes later, the *Star Wars* music theme blares upstairs, and the voices of the characters from his favorite *Star Wars* movie *The Empire Strikes Back* travel upstairs to my window. He can recite the movie in his sleep, but he crowds his mind with activity. Restless. The sound of his feet pressing against hardwood floorboards tells me his escape into fantasy and heroic deeds of iconic heroes no longer works. He sees the ploy for what it is – a mental barrier – and his body retreats.

A man faces a lion, a mugger, an enraged SUV driver on a freeway and refuses to back down and will not allow his manhood to be challenged, but the moment the villain love or emotion enters the scene, the gladiator cowers in fear shaking inside praying others cannot smell the fear or hear the pounding heart. The man, this warrior downstairs who has shared my love and my bed, faces this demon, and I do not know if he emerges as the victor or the defeated.

I hear him pace back and forth across the hardwood floor in the living room. The creak of the wood tells me he walks near the refrigerator, and then the creak of the wood tells me he walks to the kitchen table again, and I know he wrestles with eternity because some decisions are final, no rewind switch to undo damage whether intentional or not.

I hear his footsteps muffled by the carpet as he climbs the stairs to my room. I feel his presence as he stands there in the doorway. I know if I turn from the window and face him, I will see the sadness in his eyes. I turn to face him and curse myself for feeling weakness sweep over me. I want him and I know he wants me, but I steal a glance at the window. It hardens my resolve.

He walks closer to me and his feet make no sound on the brick red carpet. He wears only burgundy pajama bottoms, and I admire his fitness dedication – a habit that is hard to break from his days as a personal trainer. It shows his pride in his muscular chest — a six-pack, eight-pack washboard of muscle. I could place him on the floor, cover his body with white butcher paper, trace his body with charcoal and find that his chest will leave an imprint on the white butcher paper. Men envy his physique, and women want his embrace on nights when wind flutters curtains. On those nights, the night air wakes us, and we greet the night with smiles and watery eyes.

"I know you don't understand any of this," he says.

"Understand? What is there to understand about us except what has to be? We live separate lives from this night forward," I say making the decision seem as trivial as choosing which lipstick to wear for the day — fire engine red lipstick or orange passion lipstick. We look at each other, and I hear his whisper warm against my skin. The wind flutters the curtains, the car cranks, and the dog barks. The car drives away, and someone hits the dog. The dog howls. Neighbors say curse words. The dog stops howling, and the wind stops fluttering the curtains.

"Nicole, do you remember the day —"

I cover his mouth with my hand and love the way his black mustache feels under my fingers. "Forget yesterday. We cannot reminisce now, can we? What purpose would it serve? We don't want the same things."

I hear him sigh with sadness. He weeps too inside. His lips find mine, but there is no passion this time. Only sadness. And when he holds me, makes love to me, I wonder if the last time isn't really the best time when so much tenderness, gentleness, love, sadness, and pain fill this moment.

His rap-techno music fills the house and the neighborhood, neighbors say curse words, the dog barks again, and I allow him to hold me and watch the wind flutter the curtains. Now, the night air smells foul and sickness overwhelms me from the stupid city dump near this neighborhood. Funny, how I have never seen those dumps in the more affluent parts of town. *Oh, God, the smell hangs in the air! Please change the direction of the wind.* His mouth will not give me a release from the stink of the night air because his mouth covers my mouth again and burns my tears away.

"Turn your damn music down!"

"Call the police!"

"Dumb kids. No respect. No respect."

As if in response to our music, someone blares his rock music playing Queen's *Another One Bites the Dust,* while another neighbor parks a car in front of the house and blasts some Tejano music, but I ignore the background symphony. Radio music wars? Ridiculous.

Funky bass remix.

I hate this neighborhood. The neighbors curse, his rap-techno music fills the house, the neighbors will call the police, and the dog howls again. I allow myself to fade into his body and his music. The pound and the pulse of the music match his thrusts inside of me, the night air stinks, and I don't want the smell of anything.

My neighborhood serves as home for people who are too poor or too old to live anywhere else. Many of them have grown children who moved away and don't give a damn how their parents fare like that woman who keeps looking for her son. Another lost soul wears pink rollers in her hair looking for her cats all the time. Sometimes the teenage boys laugh, and I know they have tortured the cats again. I watch them especially the one called Rome. Why he has that name, I'll never figure out. His smile never lights up his eyes; his eyes are already dead.

I hate this neighborhood. Someone killed a kid down the street. The repeated pop pop pop of the gun and squealing tires confirmed that someone's son was another casualty. I heard he was only sixteen. Dumb. Wasteful. Gunshots firing at all hours of the night, ambulances blaring with flashing lights, teens dying, and women struggling to care for children with no fathers around plague this neighborhood.

This hopelessness chokes the night air killing the mind, the soul, and the body leaving only anger in its wake like a tornado bent on destruction. Some have weathered that tornado and other ills like the original residents who lament the decay that has eaten away at their once beautiful neighborhood. Those men and women control their anger and hold on until they hit the lottery or worse until they shoot someone's kid for intruding into their homes. When the people look at ambulances and the police cars, it's all the same story to them. No one cares because these people are not valued but feared and viewed as tomorrow's problem.

Neighbors bang on the door while others argue. I can hear the Miller family next door. When she gets mad, her English refuses to come fast enough and her Spanish flows like daggers at her *gringo* husband. He understands enough Spanish to call her an evil witch – *bruja*.

All of these malcontents, suffering people, grate under my fingernails that have not seen a manicure at the salon in so long now. Money is tight. I fix my own hair, and it shows. We had to leave our old neighborhood where children respected their parents. Here it's always the same family dramas.

Anthony told me what to expect when we found it – the burglar bars on most of the homes told me what I feared. Living here has been bearable because of Anthony, but now ... it is different now. I'm leaving this neighborhood; the movers arrive tomorrow. Anthony found another place for me and paid rent for six months. It's a nicer neighborhood, but it costs more. Six months. He told me I could handle it on my own after six months.

On my own now? I am finished. Why did I accept his generous offer? I am not a charity case.

ANTHONY STALLS AS LONG as he can by taking the last flight. The neighbors stand outside in their robes and pajamas and watch us leave. Some smoke and others hold beer cans in their hands.

"About time."

"Disturbing our neighborhood."

"Ruining my property values."

"I pay taxes not to listen to that dumb shit."

Some neighbors curse and talk about our loud music. The brown dog chases our car when we leave the street for the airport.

SMALL AIRPORTS AT NIGHT remind me of cemeteries — the ones where the dead and buried have no visitors. Their descendants have succumbed to death themselves, and they belong in quiet places where they are forgotten souls with no activity, no life. Nothing. This airport reminds me of a well-lit cemetery with no life. No one laughs. No one waits to greet a spouse. No child falls asleep in a chair with his mother. No boyfriend waits to see his girlfriend. Only us.

The night air stinks even more now, the rap-techno music cannot hide the smell, and he won't let me wear my headphones in the airport. The silence hurts my ears.

We don't talk. It's better this way. Better to accept the reality of our situation. I can deal with that. Can he deal with that? He clenches his jaw as he sits and stares at the television that bombards him with infomercials of get-rich quick schemes through real estate or gold, and those stupid beautiful-body-now shows. He owns that infomercial tape, I'm sure. I'm sick of the images, which are not loud enough like the rap-techno music that assaults with images of violation and nothingness — images of emptiness.

He has not asked for the ring back, but I will give it to him. The marquise-shaped diamond and gold band sparkle under the fluorescent lights.

Boarding call.

We stand and walk to the door leading to his flight and our separate lives. As he holds me, panic grips me. My heart beats. The silence allows everyone to hear. People stare at me, and he stares at me. Where is my rap-techno music? The noise is what I need not silence because everything happens too quickly. I catch glimpses of people walking by us to board the plane. My stomach twists in knots.

Boarding call.

The sweat rolls down my arm. I am scared, but I refuse to cry. I lift my chin, and his lips touch mine for the last time, and it reminds me of those old black-and-white movies where a woman wearing high-heeled pumps with a tiny waist says goodbye with tears in her eyes to a man leaving her forever. As the woman weeps, the man suddenly stops the train or the car, races back to the woman never letting her disappear from his life again as they kiss each other while the words The End flash across the screen in beautiful script.

The End. Movies. Romances. Whatever.

As we pull away from each other, I give him the ring. The baffled hurt in those brown eyes bothers me, he looks like the brown dog that chased our car earlier in the evening except the dog's brown eyes had anger. I play the rap-techno music loud in my mind so that he cannot hear my heart shrivel into a lifeless black organ nor hear my throat collapse upon itself to destroy the sob creating in my body. I defeat my lifeless black organ and my sob with my car vibrating, walls shaking, chest thumping, bass bumping rap-techno music in my head. Loud. I increase the music's volume.

Funky bass remix.

I break his gaze.

"So, you don't want it?" he asks me.

"Why? It symbolizes nothing for us. It's only a piece of jewelry. Besides, I can't wear it now. I'll take it to a pawn shop."

He slowly nods his head, his eyebrows knit together, and he bites his lip. He surprises me by not chastising me, but he is different now.

"I want you to understand more than anything," he says looking from me to the ring in his palm.

Funky bass remix.

It hides the pain. That's what good about my internal music. I catch a nosy, old woman staring at us while she waits to board the same flight. I glare at her, and she turns away in a huff. The old biddy. Serves her right.

"I do understand," I say.

"Then why?" he asks holding the ring.

I only stare at him. "I always thought you'd make a great father, but sometimes people want different things," I pause. "You really believe it wouldn't work, huh?"

"Nicole, in time you'll understand. I love you more for doing this," he says shoving the ring back into my hand. "I want you to keep the ring. If you ever are in a rough spot, you can get some money."

I remain quiet and fumble with my shirt pockets. He is the last passenger. He answers the final boarding call and walks away from me, and I hold my tongue to keep my resolve. I dig my nails into my palms to steady myself, and I watch the runway until his plane departs. Then I walk away.

I walk alone in the airport. It slowly dies. The smell of burnt popcorn lingers in the air, the cigarette butts smolder to ashes, and the janitors remove the trash. The stink of the popcorn, the stink of the ashes, and the stink of the night air that once smelled sweet burns my nostrils. My heart, a shriveled, lifeless black organ, tries to reassert itself, but I become the champion again, and it shrinks at my anger. The sob tries to escape past my throat, but my throat collapses even tighter and the sob dies. It cannot breathe. I insert the rap-techno music in the CD player of my mind, press the repeat button, and wonder why did the wind wake me?

———◉———

FUNKY BASS REMIX.

The Calling

Toni threw the Bible at her husband. He ducked, and the black, leather-bound book sailed over his head knocking the seven white porcelain angels from the shelf behind him. The angels fell on the royal blue carpet without breaking.

"Is it true, Malcolm? You're only telling me this to mess with me, right?" Toni said with her hands on her hips. One red snakeskin pump lay on the floor behind her husband, and the other red snakeskin pump remained on her foot. She limped towards her husband who kneeled on one knee the way he had when he proposed to her.

"Malcolm, answer me."

Her husband glanced up at her then lowered his head as he retrieved the Bible from the floor. "Toni, I've been called and —"

"Damn it, I don't want to hear that 'I've been called' crap," she said interrupting him. Limping closer to him, Toni removed her pump from her brown-hosed foot and held it in her hand.

"Toni, I've been called to the ministry. I'm going to preach God's word," he said. He rose from the floor and put his black suit jacket on over his white starched long-sleeved shirt and red tie. "I'm going to be a preacher, and that means you're going to be a preacher's wife."

Narrowing her brown eyes, Toni threw the other red snakeskin pump at her husband and missed again. He walked past her. "I'll pray for you at church today."

"Pray? That's your answer to everything," Toni said walking behind her husband who towered above her. "I didn't sign up to be a preacher's wife."

The door slammed, and Toni threw her hands up in frustration and banged her head against the front door three times. She heard his Ford Expedition pull from the driveway. Sighing, Toni sat on the mahogany coffee table in her short-sleeved red dress. Her matching straw hat lay on the couch. The grandfather clock ticked, and she glanced at the bronze praying hands that hung on the wall. Underneath the praying hands was a brief prayer.

She put her hat on her head, placed her red snakeskin pumps on her feet, and left the five-bedroom house. She studied her black four-door sedan Mercedes out front and the green manicured lawn. Retrieving her spare King James Bible from underneath the front passenger seat, Toni drove to church.

———◈———

TONI WORKED AS A VICE president for the communications department for CBYT Toys. Communicating was her business. Toni's fingers punched and pressed the buttons and digital keypad on her palm pilot, her cordless telephone, her cell phone, and her laptop. Her fingers gripped blue ink executive pens and scribbled notes on yellow pads of paper. While driving, Toni heard her phone beep. She picked it up and read the text message. *Carlton and Reeves Co. finalized merger. Will provide new product. Ready for official announcement. See you Monday. CJ*

Placing the phone on her lap and pulling the sedan-sized Mercedes into Pine Creek Avenue Missionary Baptist Church's parking lot, Toni drove past the reserved parking spots for the church pastor and the pastor's wife who both drove matching his and her champagne-colored Cadillacs. Toni drove around the full parking lot filled with Volvos, BMWs, Cadillacs, Jaguars, SUVs, Dodge Rams and Ford F-150 trucks. She found a space between a black Lexus and a white Volvo. Walking into the church, Toni nodded at the other latecomers who arrived when she did. She glanced at her watch. Eleven-thirty. Toni hadn't missed all of the choir's gospel singing. She wanted to hear at least three songs before the ministers started their praying and preaching sessions.

Entering the sanctuary, Toni saw the black choir, dressed in burgundy robes accented with white trim around the collars, and the black congregation standing in a group song. Some church members clapped their hands and sang. A few women shouted, and women ushers ran to their aid with handheld cardboard fans stapled to wooden sticks. Other male ushers with firm, but gentle hands restrained some of the women to prevent them from hurting themselves as they threw their hands in the air, jumped up and down in the pews, and dropped to the red-carpet floor or benches. One deacon carried a woman who fainted.

The Spirit was moving today, her husband would say. She hoped Malcolm didn't get too filled with the Spirit and start hollering and strutting his holy dance in the aisle. Instead, she found her husband standing, singing and clapping his hands. She sat beside him on the red cushioned pew. He saw her, but nothing distracted him when the Spirit moved him, he once told her. He sat down on the pew, smiled revealing his straight white teeth, and nodded his head to the music. He jumped up again and clapped his hands and closed his eyes.

"Amen!" he said. "Say it now. Thank you, Jesus!"

Toni shook her head and crossed her arms. A few minutes later she opened her black straw purse, removed her notebook and blue executive pen, and wrote down key points that needed to be addressed in the news release for the new toy supplier.

"Amen, Lord," he said.

Toni's pen slid across the blue-lined yellow pad and filled it with her plans in blue ink.

———◉———

TONI NODDED HER HEAD as the gospel music with its organ, piano, drums, guitars, and keyboard sounds floated around the huge congregation. Her husband reminded her of a jack-in-the-box with his frequent sitting and jumping and clapping. She rolled her eyes thankful that the huge, red-brimmed hat hid her face. When he finally sat down, he took her hand and squeezed it. She looked at his brown hand against her own brown hand and returned his smile.

She wanted to forget their morning argument. He was unaware of the pot roast she had simmering for him at home. Despite her career and her schedule, she remembered how to make a home cooked Sunday dinner. Today, they'd eat her food instead of a meal cooked at a restaurant by a pair of unfamiliar hands. Today she wasn't Toni Washington, vice president of CBYT Toys. Today she was simply Toni Jones, Malcolm Jones' wife. She held his hand tighter.

After the pastor delivered his sermon and opened the church for membership, Toni leaned back against the pew and stretched her legs. Dinner.

The pot roast, mashed potatoes, and seasoned green beans made her mouth water. Did they have dessert at home?

Toni smiled and glanced at her husband who stood up, left the pew, and walked down the red-carpet aisle towards the pastor's outstretched hands. Toni's mouth dropped open, and she gripped the pew in front of her.

"Don't do this, Malcolm," she pleaded in a whisper drowned out by the organ's gospel music. The organ's hollow tones, once pleasant, now sounded like a phantom's macabre music. The organ howled louder as her husband approached the bench in front of the congregation. Its hollow sounds, hungry and evil now to her ears, cast its spell on her husband drawing him near like a crack addict with a twenty-dollar bill to the drug dealer who waited on the corner by the telephone pole. This crack dealer, this organ player with his phantom music, now cast its net like a spider and her husband was leaving her for its web. She looked at the empty seat beside her and again at her husband who stood in front of the eleven o'clock service congregation of nearly three thousand members.

"God bless you, brother," said a minister who shook Malcolm's hand.

Two men and three women stood beside Malcolm. The two men — a father and son — wanted church membership and to be baptized for the first time. The church congregation responded with amen. After the invitation to discipleship ended, a minister passed a microphone to each woman who all requested prayer. When the microphone passed from the third woman to Malcolm, Toni placed her purse strap on her shoulder.

"I'm thankful for everything the Lord has blessed me with today and all my life," Malcolm said.

Toni removed her keys from her black straw purse.

"I'm thankful for my wife and my fellow church members," Malcolm said.

Toni pulled her huge, red-brimmed hat down further on her head.

"I want to announce my calling into the ministry. The Lord's been calling me a long time, and well ... I'm here."

The church congregation cheered and shouts of amen and hallelujah rang from the pews, and some church members stood in celebration. The organ shouted its triumph and throngs of people leaned and rocked from side to side as the music swept them away again. Toni stood with them, glanced at her husband, and vacated the sanctuary. She walked down the red carpet and exited the church building. Passing by the pastor's reserved parking spot, Toni found her house key and scratched a twelve-inch-long mark on his champagne-colored Cadillac.

<hr>

TONI SAT AT HER KITCHEN table and ate her pot roast alone in the dark house without lights and without a sun that disappeared behind clouds increasing the darkness inside the house. Toni wiped her mouth with her napkin. Pushing her plate aside, Toni made her husband's plate of pot roast, mashed potatoes, and seasoned green beans, covered it with another plate, and stuck it in the microwave. She sat in the dark at the kitchen table and listened to the kitchen clock tick tick tick.

<hr>

TONI WORKED IN HER home office on news releases. She sat at her computer rereading the news release again on her iMac grey computer. She scrolled down the screen looking at the print in Helvetica type, a skinny type that read easily. She inserted another paragraph into the news release when her husband knocked on the door.

"Toni?" he said, poking his head in and Toni glanced up from her computer and smiled.

Malcolm held a yellow legal pad in his hands. "Toni, I want you to read it. These are notes for my first sermon. You're good with words."

He handed the yellow legal pad in his hands to Toni.

She stared at the yellow legal pad a moment than glanced up at Malcolm who beamed like a child on Christmas Day receiving his gifts before sunrise. Toni took her red pen in her hands and placed the yellow pad on her desk. She read the first sentence and then the black cordless phone on her desk rang.

"Don't answer it, Toni," Malcolm said as he leaned forward in the chair.

"It'll just take a minute. It's probably the office." Toni answered the phone, pushed the yellow pad away from her on the desk and swiveled around in her chair to face the computer screen.

"Yes, sir. You don't like your comment? Okay. We can change it right now. Give me your quote." Toni typed as she held the phone between her ear and shoulder.

Malcolm waited a few minutes then grabbed the yellow legal pad containing his sermon notes. Malcolm stood up, grabbed the yellow pad from her desk, and left Toni's office with a scowl.

SEVERAL WEEKS LATER, Toni's husband would deliver his first sermon.

Malcolm insisted on the two of them riding to Sunday evening service together. She nodded and climbed into the Ford Expedition next to him.

"You will sit on the third pew with the other ministers' wives this evening," he said as he drove to the church. "Tonight you will be my loving wife who supports me."

Toni reached into her purse and removed her cell phone and palm pilot. Malcolm leaned over and with his right hand jerked the cell phone and palm pilot from her hands and tossed both devices into the back seat. He returned his right hand to the wheel of the car.

"Tonight, you will not be Vice President Toni Washington, but you will be the other half to Rev. Malcolm Jones — Mrs. Jones. Understand?"

"Yes, Malcolm. Honor and obey," Toni murmured as she stared out the windows. As they approached the church, Toni drummed her fingers in her lap. She needed air, but Malcolm locked the windows. She reached for the air vent and lowered the temperature to a cooler degree. He stared at her from the corner of his eyes, but she ignored him. He came prepared with *his* tools, she noted seeing his black King James Bible, small gold cross, gospel CDs and his notes on a yellow legal pad for his first sermon.

Once they entered the church, Toni swallowed and brushed her sweaty palms against her blue skirt. Her feet dragged across the red carpet and her legs felt weighted with iron. She glanced at her black pumps and shook her head.

The sanctuary hallways narrowed, and she reached out and touched the walls that caved in around her. She glimpsed at her husband who hummed the old gospel hymn *Amazing Grace,* but he did not return her gaze. Frustrated,

Toni studied the gold-framed photos of the original founders of the church, which included several women.

Toni and Malcolm reached the wooden brown double doors of the sanctuary. She stopped and turned around, but her husband put his arm around her back and escorted her inside the sanctuary. Toni glanced at the pews in the back where she normally sought refuge. She wanted to run, but Malcolm's grip restrained her. She stiffened when Malcolm led her to the pew for ministers' wives and left her with the women who greeted her.

Defeated, Toni saw the sanctuary fill with men, women, teenagers, and children. Their murmured conversation and laughter filled the sanctuary. The musicians walked in from the right side of the sanctuary. The drummer tapped the cymbals, the guitar player picked plucked a few chords, and the keyboard player thumped a few notes on his keyboard. Watching her husband approach the podium, Toni lowered her head and stared at her unopened Bible.

———◉———

HIS VOICE ROSE AND fell several times, and he maintained eye contact with his audience keeping their attention. He glanced at her several times and smiled. Toni glanced around the room and saw people nod their heads while others clapped their hands.

One man even stood up, clapped his hands and spoke. "Amen! Say it brother!" Other voices met the man's comment with approval.

Toni swallowed and gripped the Bible tighter. She smiled. Her husband always had a way with telling stories with the way his hands waved in the air, and the way he walked around the podium. Dressed in his navy suit, her husband looked like he belonged in a corporate board room, which he did, but seeing him with his hand against the podium and hearing him drive home the point of his sermon of living for Jesus Christ, she realized that he belonged there leading as a minister.

He belonged there leading as a minister.

He was on his way to having his own church.

Toni panicked. Her husband was on to having something else too. Many of the women leaned forward adjusting their dresses, fumbling with their suits and wiping imaginary lint, and fidgeting in their chairs. Some licked their red and grape and fuchsia-colored lips hungry waiting for a shrimp cocktail with wine to be delivered to them. Yeah, licking their lips hungry like a cat in heat, hungry for a man, hungry for a preacher man, hungry for a fallible man in a suit claiming to follow God. Yeah, these hungry sisters wanted to test to see how devoted to God his calling was. And so, they crossed their legs, pulled at their skirts and wiped the lint that wasn't there from their clothes.

He belonged there leading as a minister.

He was on his way to having his own church.

He was on his way to having something else — his fan club, his groupies. Malcolm now joined the ranks of professional athletes and singers who had groupies in every town ready to snatch their panties off, if they wore any, to give a man his one dream with the hopes that his seed implanted itself within her giving her a guaranteed meal ticket nine months later for eighteen years. Toni frowned as she heard the wheels spin in those women's heads —their thoughts so loud everyone in the congregation could have heard their schemes. Even the wood creaked and groaned at their foul thoughts.

She glanced at her husband again. Malcolm, who was on his way to having his own church, was on to having something else too — his ready-made fan club. He didn't need the basketball, the football, the golf club, the microphone, the rap contract, the Mercedes. All he needed was his Bible, his proclamation of being a minister, and a nice car, and he had his ready-made fan club.

Silly women, Toni thought as she watched them. They better move around to the next victim.

AFTER THE SERMON, EVERYONE congratulated him on his sermon. Toni hung back in the pews standing and observing everything. Women shook his hand, and some embraced his hand like ham and turkey meat between slices of wheat and rye bread hands smiling and glad to have a minister who made them feel God's word.

Finally, he looked up and waved to her and she smiled as he put his arm around her introducing her to his fan club. Toni heard the invitations to dinner for them and wanting to know the couple better. Toni smiled as she watched the women in their red hats and black hats and orange hats and pink hats and natural hats and yellow hats and blue hats. They shook her hand and expressed their approval of her husband, Rev. Jones. Some women and men shook her hands with firm grips around hands that worked hard fields many days while other hands soft and manicured revealed no blisters and the gnarled hands, also soft, sported diamonds that blinded in the church's light. Some of the men hobbled by on black canes curved like red and white candy canes at Christmas while some escorted women away in wheelchairs and smiles covering their faces as they rode the wheelchairs like chariots leading them to a new land. And these people, these church people, welcomed her.

"Sister Jones, God is with him today."

"Sister Jones, you should come to our home for dinner."

"God bless Rev. and Sister Jones."

Toni sighed.

ONE SATURDAY AFTERNOON at one p.m., the doorbell rang, and Toni opened the door and frowned. Standing on her porch were seven ministers' wives from the church. Toni, wearing her black bike shorts, and red sleeveless tank, pulled her bike onto the porch. Her husband, now that he entered the ministerial ranks, attended theology school on Saturdays.

"Hello. You're the ladies from church. How can I help you?"

"Toni Jones?"

"Yes?"

"We're the ministers' wives from the church," said a woman with gray hair pulled in a bun. Her round glasses nearly covered her face. "We've come to officially welcome you to our group. Rev. Jones said we should come by today. Didn't he tell you?"

Toni ignored the woman's question and watched the women melt under the sun in their crème suits. She sipped water from her water bottle. "Listen, I'd love to chat, but I'm late for my bike ride. Is there any special reason why you came?"

"We want to let you know that as a wife of a minister, you'll be watched closely just like your husband."

"Excuse me, watched?"

"I mean," said the older woman, "that people outside the church and inside the church will expect a higher moral standard from you. People will look at you and make judgments about your husband."

Some women nodded, some women said amen, and some women fanned themselves with paper fans from a local funeral home with Martin Luther King Jr.'s face plastered over it.

"I see," Toni said watching the brown-and-bronze makeup slide off the women's faces in tiny brown and bronze beads. Their black shoes covered their feet, and their dresses hid their legs.

"And that means we have to give you the rules of behavior," the leader said. She reached into her black tote bag and handed Toni a red folder. "Visit us at the church Wednesday night to discuss these handouts and anything else you have questions about."

"Yes," said another woman, "that is if your *career* will allow it."

"Well, I'll check my calendar. Look, it's been nice, but I've got to run now."

Toni rolled her bike off the porch past the women. She pedaled away from the women with their crème suits, matching hosiery, and sweating faces behind.

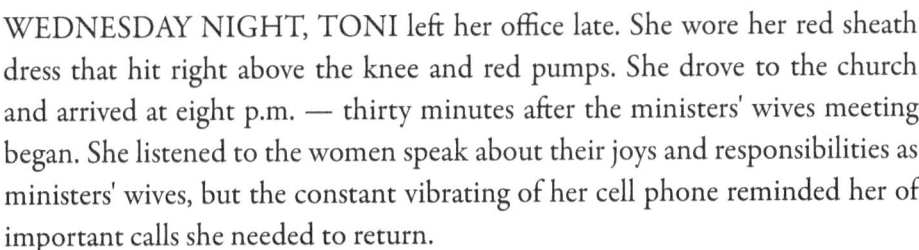

WEDNESDAY NIGHT, TONI left her office late. She wore her red sheath dress that hit right above the knee and red pumps. She drove to the church and arrived at eight p.m. — thirty minutes after the ministers' wives meeting began. She listened to the women speak about their joys and responsibilities as ministers' wives, but the constant vibrating of her cell phone reminded her of important calls she needed to return.

She half remembered what the women said, but only knew that the weak red fruit punch and stale butter cookies they offered left her mouth craving red wine and a slice of Southern bourbon pecan pie. Besides, the CEO of the new toy product wanted to have a conference call tomorrow afternoon; he disliked the news release wording.

"Toni Jones?"

"Yes," she replied. The meeting had ended, and Toni's thoughts were once again lost in work. She stood and shook hands with the woman, the one who made the snide remarks about her career and time commitments last Saturday. "Thank you for inviting me."

"Yes," the woman said, pulling her aside. "Toni, my sister, appearance is also important as a minister's wife. They touched on it a little bit tonight, but I'll be even more blunt. Your dresses are too short for being a minister's wife. Perhaps you should wear career attire for work only."

"What?" Toni said taking a step back from the woman. Her eyes widened, and she rubbed her chin as she studied the woman's mouth curl in a crooked smile.

"That's why the women don't sit on the first pew. We don't want to create lustful situations for the men, you know. We don't want them to sin and have ungodly thoughts." The woman touched Toni's shoulder.

"What's wrong with my dresses?" Toni said. She shrugged the woman's hand from her shoulder and placed her hands on her hips.

"Well, you're at church, not work, and it doesn't look good, you know," the woman smiled revealing brown smoker-stained teeth.

Toni pointed her finger in the woman's face. "I bet my dress will really look short if you were laid out on this floor," she said. "Watch your step, sister. The last time I checked you weren't paying the bills at my house."

Toni turned on her heel and left the woman.

Several other ministers' wives went to their comrade's aid and listened as she recanted her encounter with Toni. Their comments fell on Toni's ears as she left their meeting room.

"I can't believe she's acting like that. Lord."

"See some people are so high and mighty."

"Bless Rev. Jones. She's going to be a problem."

"Keep praying for her."

"She's in God's house, not her corporate board room."

Toni walked to the darkened parking lot, turned on the car's CD player, and blared a Lenny Kravitz CD.

───────◦───────

TWO HOURS LATER TONI read the reports on CBYT Toys Toni heard the front door slam. Her husband hadn't bothered to park his SUV in the garage. She sipped her wine and ignored his heavy footsteps on the carpet. She scribbled some notes in red ink on her reports and sipped more wine. Malcolm burst into her office with his red tie loosened. Toni watched him stand in the doorway. She stopped working on her reports.

"Toni, did you have to point your finger in the woman's face?"

"She tried to tell me what I should wear," Toni said putting her reports down on the mahogany wood desk. "She was out of line with me."

"No, you were out of line," he said, pointing a finger at her. "Everybody's talking about you. They're whispering about me behind my back saying I can't control my house or you. You're making me look bad."

Toni leaned back in her black leather high-backed chair. She folded her fingers into a church steeple. She smiled. "I'm making you look bad?"

"Toni, you're not acting like ... like," he stammered.

"A minister's wife?" She crossed her chest with her arms and narrowed her eyes. "I didn't ask to be a minister's wife, remember? You forced this on me, Malcolm. And now you expect me to change the way I behave and dress just because I'm a minister's wife?" she paused, and her voice softened. "Malcolm, you told me once that you liked the way I dressed and my attitude. You said I had spirit."

Malcolm stood in the doorway holding the brass doorknob. He said nothing but stared at her. He closed the door and Toni heard his muffled footsteps on the stairs again. She heard the front door open and close as she sat there in front of her computer and listened to his SUV spin away from the driveway.

———— ⬤ ————

WHEN SHE WOKE UP THE next morning, she saw that her husband never slept in the bed with her that night.

———— ⬤ ————

TONI CAME HOME FROM work one day and found her husband in the living room sitting on the floor looking through albums. Red, blue, and black albums surrounded him on the blue carpet. He smiled as he looked at the photos and Toni watched him.

"Going down memory lane?" she offered as she entered the living room.

"Yeah, I guess you could say that," he said as he stared at one photo. He handed the photo to Toni.

She starred at the photo of the man and woman seated at a dinner table at some function. The woman smiled from the photo.

"Those are my grandparents, Rev. and Mrs. David Wilson. He told me I was going to be a preacher man when I was ten years old." Malcolm said. "He and my grandmother were married a long time, and they seemed happy."

Malcolm became quiet and resumed his digging of old photos and memories.

Toni glanced at the photo again and returned it to Malcolm. She stood a few minutes then left the living room and Malcolm sitting on the blue carpet floor with his memories.

———◆———

"TONI I WAS ACCEPTED at the seminary school. I start taking classes in the fall. Maybe we can have a vacation, attend the Baptists convention, and make a two-week vacation. What do you think?"

"A church convention? For a week? Malcolm that's the same week the media professionals' conference in Washington, D.C. takes place. Maybe you can come with me."

"Toni, I really want you come to the convention with me. It would mean a lot to me."

"Maybe next year. I already made my travel arrangements for the media conference," she said as she closed her planner. "Besides, we can have fun and catch up with some people in D.C. What do you think?"

"You've already made plans, so continue with your trip. I'll go ahead and go to the church convention. I think it will be good for me to be there."

———◆———

FOR TWO YEARS, MALCOLM spent more time at Pine Creek Avenue Missionary Baptist Church, while Toni spent more time at work. One day, Malcolm called Toni at work and said they needed to talk about his ministry decision. Toni smiled when she received her husband's message, and she left work early and found him at home waiting for her.

She went into the living room and saw him staring at the seven white porcelain angels that rested on the shelf. He picked up one angel and examined the white porcelain figurine before placing it on the shelf again never looking up when she entered the room.

"Hi, Malcolm."

"Toni."

"So, what's the big thing?" Toni said snapping her fingers.

Malcolm turned around and faced her. His reddened eyes surprised her. She walked closer to him and placed her hands on his arms. "Malcolm, what's wrong?"

Her husband laughed a moment then looked at her again. "You were right. I shouldn't have forced you to be a minister's wife."

Toni's lips lifted in a smile. *Yes! Amen! Hallelujah!*

"Toni, I need a wife who will be a minister's wife and a helper to me."

"What are you talking about? I do help you. I make sure that this house is together, and I critique your sermons and-"

Malcolm smiled and shook his head. "Toni, I know you think you're helping, but you've been fighting me about this for years. I'm not asking you to compete with me. I want a woman who God will also call to be a minister's wife," he paused. "Maybe He didn't call you, and then maybe He did, and you are rebelling. Doesn't matter now, because that's not what I need."

Toni's smile fell. She watched her husband go into their kitchen, and her stomach tightened. She blinked back tears. "Malcolm?" She tried to control her wavering voice.

"Toni, it's time to move on for both of us," he said from the kitchen. "This way you can always be Toni Washington, executive and not Toni Jones, the rebellious minister's wife."

"What?" She mumbled.

Toni's body landed on the coffee table with a thud. She stared at the royal blue carpet and waited. Her husband remained in the kitchen fumbling with dishes, glasses, pots, and pans. She heard flatware clink in the sink. Toni drummed her fingers on the table and waited for Malcolm to finish talking to her. Finally, Toni jumped up and paced back and forth in the living room.

Malcolm hummed another gospel hymn she had heard once before, but he remained in the kitchen fumbling with his dishes and ignoring her. Staring at the white porcelain angels on the shelf in front of her, Toni picked them up, and smashed them against the wall.

Don't miss out!

Visit the website below and you can sign up to receive emails whenever Michele Majors publishes a new book. There's no charge and no obligation.

https://books2read.com/r/B-A-TMTP-XKQRB

BOOKS 2 READ

Connecting independent readers to independent writers.

About the Author

Michele Majors is a writer, poet, and author of the fiction collection *The Bond*.

Her love for writing began at an early age, and her parents encouraged and nurtured this interest. As a child and teen, she loved creating and sharing stories with her siblings and friends. As a child, she often played television reporter and interviewed her friends.

In college, she channeled that writing interest to pursue a journalism career. She earned a bachelor's degree in journalism from the University of North Texas, and a master's degree in humanities from The University of Texas at Dallas. Later in her career, she earned a master's of business administration from Concordia University-Portland. She has worked as a news reporter, magazine managing editor, and a communications director.

After she covered her work assignments during the day or special events and meetings at night, she spent her free time writing fiction and poetry. She was one of six finalists for the Naomi Long Madgett Poetry Award in 2002. Her fiction, poetry, and op-eds have appeared in *The Centrifugal Eye, KenteCloth: Southwest Voices of the African Diaspora, KenteCloth: African American Voices in Texas, New Texas '94*, and *The Dallas Morning News*.

When she is not writing, she enjoys spending time with her family and her dog. She is the author of *Revolution*, a collection of poetry.

www.ingramcontent.com/pod-product-compliance
Lightning Source LLC
Chambersburg PA
CBHW060405030726
47497CB00003B/861